HASHTAG:
IT'S COMPLICATED

HASHTAG:
IT'S COMPLICATED

RITU KHURANA

PAPER TOWNS
PUBLISHERS

PAPER TOWNS
PUBLISHERS

First published by 2025

Papertowns Publishers
72, Vishwanath Dham Colony,
Niwaru Road, Jhotwara,
Jaipur, 302012

Hashtag: It's Complicated

ISBN Print Book – 978-93-6185-231-2

For permissions, inquiries, or other information, contact: ritu.author@gmail.com; or visit: www.ritukhurana.in

Printed in India

With the blessings of the Almighty

ॐ नमः शिवाय

Aum Namah Shivaay

ACKNOWLEDGEMENT

This book is dedicated, first and foremost, to my grandfather, **Sham Lal Khurana**—a man whose life embodied discipline, resilience, and quiet brilliance. A true self-made visionary, he rebuilt his world after the Partition, laying the foundations of both his business and our family in New Delhi while always finding ways to give back to the community.

Though widely known as an entrepreneur and philanthropist, at his core, he was a poet—a man moved by language, rhythm, and emotion. **That love for words was my first inheritance**, and I credit him with the spark that ignited my writing journey.

Thank you, **Lalaji**, for your unwavering blessings—always felt, always guiding me from above and beyond.

To my parents—thank you for your unconditional love, your support through every high and low, and for always standing by my dreams, even when they didn't always make sense.

To the friends who believed in me more than I believed in myself—you know who you are. Your encouragement, your faith, your late-night pep talks, and endless rereads helped bring this story to life.

To my family, who kept me grounded when I drifted and taught me how to listen—not just to what's said, but to everything in between. Your quiet presence and deep insights helped me shape this story with heart.

And finally, to the eternal romantic in me—and in millions like me across the world—who still believe in second chances and happily ever afters. This one's for us.

May we always keep dreaming.

CONTENTS

CHAPTER ONE

A NEW BEGINNING

Angad Sareen had spent the last decade and a half pretending he didn't miss home.

New York had its allure—the city that never slept had kept him moving, had kept him distracted. The relentless energy, the towering skyline, the rush of ambition that pulsed through its streets—it had been intoxicating at first. There, he had built an empire in the media world, launching digital news platforms and print magazines that people actually wanted to read. He had crafted himself into a man who mattered, a man who dictated narratives rather than merely existing within them. He had made decisions that shaped public discourse, influenced trends, and altered corporate fortunes.

And yet, for all its glittering promise, the city never truly felt like home.

Angad left Delhi right after college, eager to carve out a future on his own terms. He had always known he wanted more—more than what his family's comfortable but predictable life could offer, more than the legacy his father had built in real estate. Business was in his blood, but he had never wanted to follow a path already paved for him. Instead, he set his sights on something bigger, something that would be entirely his own.

Getting into the best university for marketing and finance in the US had been his first real victory. He thrived there, excelling in an environment that valued sharp thinking and relentless drive. He had worked harder than most, refusing to let himself be outpaced. While others partied, he networked. While others coasted on privilege, he strategized. Every internship, every project, every late-night discussion with visiting CEOs—it had all been fuel, shaping him into the man he would become.

Moving to New York had been the natural next step. The city was a battlefield for the ambitious, and he had entered it with nothing but a sharp mind and a hunger for success. He started small—freelance consulting for media startups, leveraging his insights into digital consumer behavior. The shift from print to digital had been inevitable, and he had seen it coming long before traditional publishing and media houses did. He had capitalized on that gap, creating platforms that blended quality journalism with modern, interactive storytelling. Investors had taken notice, and soon, he wasn't just advising businesses—he was running his own.

He built a name, a reputation. His publications weren't just profitable; they were influential. His name carried weight in boardrooms, and his opinions shaped industry trends. He made money, power, and success look effortless.

But the skyscrapers and endless neon lights had never really belonged to him.

There had been moments—on the rare, quiet mornings when he stood in his Upper East Side apartment, looking down at Manhattan—that he had felt a strange kind of emptiness there. From this height, the city felt suspended in time—Central Park lay below like a dark, breathing forest framed by the soft glow of morning lights, while the skyline beyond rose in sharp lines and shimmered with the first touch of sun. The distant river gleamed silver under the pale sky, bridges faint but steady in the haze. Even the chaos felt orderly from here—cars moved like flickers of light, and the muffled city hum couldn't touch the stillness of this view. It was a view made for people who never needed to chase anything—they'd already arrived. The noise, the crowds, the constant movement had filled his days, but they hadn't filled him.

New York had given him everything he thought he had wanted.

But it was not home. It was not New Delhi.

His return to India had not been part of the plan. But life had a way of forcing change upon a man, whether he was ready for it or not.

There were days when he wondered if, in chasing all that, he had lost something, too.

Home.

Roots.

Belonging.

Himself. Or at least the version of himself who once believed success would be enough.

Gurugram, now home to Angad, had changed too. What was once a satellite town of New Delhi had become the National Capital Region's nerve center of ambition, affluence, and relentless drive.

It was a transformation he hadn't witnessed firsthand. When he had left, it was still called *Gurgaon*—its promise still unfurling. The skyline had transformed, skyscrapers gleaming under the Indian sun, promising the very same hustle and desire that had defined his years in New York.

Gurugram was no longer just a place for business; it had become a city where wealth wasn't a privilege—it was a given. Luxury cars swerved down roads that had once been humble while exclusive clubs and high-end restaurants catered to an elite who thrived on influence.

It was fast, sharp, and full of restless energy. Like Angad himself, in some ways.

This wasn't the city he had left. It wasn't the city he had imagined returning to. Yet, standing in the penthouse he now called home, he could feel a shift. The Golf Course Estate, where he now resided, was one of the most expensive neighborhoods in the country, a world apart from the chaotic yet familiar streets of Delhi where he had grown up.

Still, beneath all the gloss and glitter, Gurugram pulsed with raw, restless energy—always chasing, never settling. A city forever wanting more.

Much like the man who had returned to it.

Angad had moved back just over a month ago, but tonight, he finally allowed himself to truly feel it—he was home. Not just in body, but in spirit. The weight of the past, the choices that had led him here, finally caught up with him.

He had wanted a fresh start for himself and for his five-year-old twins.

A chance to rebuild, to create a life where they could feel a sense of belonging. More than anything, he wanted them to grow up connected to their culture, to understand the roots that ran deeper than the skyscrapers surrounding them.

But it was proving to be an uphill task.

The twins, Avik and Anika, were still adjusting to their new surroundings. Their new school, the unfamiliar culture, and the absence of Mrs. D, the nanny they had grown attached to in New York, weighed on them in ways Angad hadn't fully anticipated. They were used to the cold efficiency of Manhattan, the structured routine that had defined their young lives. Here, everything was different—the language, the food, and the people.

They acted out in small but telling ways. Bedtime had become a nightly battle, filled with protests, delayed trips to the bathroom, and sudden, urgent questions about the universe that couldn't wait until morning. Mealtimes were worse. They picked at their food, wrinkling their noses at home-cooked *dal* and *roti*, longing for the mac and cheese or chicken nuggets they had once devoured without a second thought. And then there were their stuffed toys—worn-out plush animals that had traveled across continents with them. They clung to them desperately, as if the soft fabric could tether them to the life they had left behind.

Angad understood. He, too, was still finding his footing, still figuring out how to bridge the gap between the life he had built abroad and the one he was trying to create here. He had made this move for them, for a fresh start, for stability. But stability didn't come overnight. It came in moments—small, hesitant steps toward something new.

The kids were fast asleep in their room, exhausted from their first few days at school. SLK International had come highly recommended—not for the pedigree of its students, but for the way it nurtured children, allowing them to grow beyond the weight of their surnames. That had been the only thing that mattered to Angad. His children deserved stability, an environment where they wouldn't be defined by their last name or the wealth attached to it. They needed more than what he had growing up—a childhood untouched by the shadows of ambition and expectation.

A knock at the door pulled him from his thoughts.

"Sir, your coffee."

Angad turned to see Lata, the housekeeper, placing a steaming cup on the table near the window. She was in her mid-fifties, efficient and discreet, and came with glowing references. She ran the household seamlessly, ensuring everything functioned without a hitch, yet she kept a professional distance, never overstepping boundaries.

"Thanks, Lata. The kids?"

"Fast asleep. Anika was mumbling something in her sleep before she drifted off. Avik, as usual, refused to let go of that stuffed dinosaur."

Angad allowed himself a small smile. "And Raju? Is he still on his mission to Americanize their meals?"

Lata chuckled. "He tried making mac and cheese again today. Anika said it was 'okay, but not New York okay.' I think she broke his heart a little."

Angad huffed out a quiet laugh. "Poor guy. He'll learn soon enough."

As he took a sip of his coffee, his eyes drifted back to the skyline. The city spread out before him, gleaming and endless. Delhi wasn't the same city he had left, but neither was he the same man who had once called it home.

This was a new beginning. A clean slate.

Or at least, that's what he told himself.

***

CHAPTER TWO

REVA'S WORLD

Reva Khanna sipped her coffee as she skimmed through the latest batch of edits on her tablet, her fingers absently tracing the rim of her mug. The comforting aroma of freshly brewed coffee filled her sleek, modern apartment—her sanctuary. The walls were lined with bookshelves overflowing with novels, some worn at the edges from repeated reads, others freshly stacked, waiting to be explored. The soft glow of warm lighting made the space feel cozy despite its contemporary design.

Reva was a highly sought-after freelance consultant with an MBA specializing in digital media from a reputed university in the US. She was one of the best in her field—an expert in helping businesses refine their online presence, strategize their digital content, and create compelling narratives that engaged audiences. Companies across industries valued her insight, and her reputation for delivering results had made her one of the top professionals in her domain. She had the flexibility to choose her clients, her projects, and her hours. It was a career she had built on her own terms, and she took immense pride in it.

Yet, despite her success in digital media, her heart truly lay elsewhere. Books. Reading and editing manuscripts. The rhythm of a well-crafted sentence, the intricacies of storytelling—those were her true loves. If left to her own devices, she would rather spend her days lost in a world of words than in marketing analytics and engagement metrics. Her guilty pleasure, even now, was romance novels. She devoured them in stolen moments, indulging in fictional love stories even when her own had left her wary and cautious. It was ironic, really. The hopeless romantic in her had been bruised and battered, but she couldn't stop believing in love, at least in the pages of a book.

Her work kept her busy, but she enjoyed it. Stories, words, ideas—they were her escape. Her safe haven. She had spent years cultivating a life of quiet independence, a carefully balanced blend between her work, solitude, and the responsibilities that came with her last name.

Being a 'Khanna' in the NCR, the National Capital Region of Delhi, meant expectations. The SLK International Schools, one of the city's most prestigious institutions, bore the initials of her grandfather, Sham Lal Khanna, a visionary who had built an empire of education after arriving in Delhi from Lahore during the partition, with nothing but determination. Though she had no formal role in the school's day-to-day affairs, she was still deeply involved, especially in its junior branch. It was her way of honoring her grandfather's legacy while maintaining a career that was entirely her own.

Despite her success, insecurities lingered beneath the surface. At thirty-two, she had learned to embrace her curves, but there were days when self-doubt crept in. Growing up in a world that glorified a certain body type had left scars. The sting of past rejections, particularly the one that had shattered her trust, hadn't fully faded. Her last relationship had ended with cruel finality—her fiancé leaving her for someone younger, slimmer, more conventionally beautiful. That betrayal had reinforced every childhood fear she had about never being enough.

Not that she let anyone see the cracks. Outwardly, she was confident, poised, and fiercely independent. She had learned to mask her vulnerabilities behind a sharp wit and an even sharper intellect. It was easier that way.

She lived alone in her sun-drenched, ninth-floor apartment in Ateliers, one of Gurugram's most upscale residential complexes within the vast Golf Course Estate. It was her haven, her space to breathe. Yet, she wasn't entirely on her own. Her parents lived in the same building, just a couple of floors below, ever-present yet respectful of her independence. Her mother, of course, wished she'd just move back downstairs.

"Why pay extra maintenance when we're right here?" her mother often argued. But Reva needed this. The physical separation, no matter how minor, was a boundary she valued.

She wasn't completely antisocial, though. Weekends often meant family dinners, catching up with her cousins, or entertaining her closest friends over wine and cheese. But at the end of the day, she returned to a bed that was hers alone, a silence that belonged solely to her.

The morning sun streamed through the large windows, bathing her apartment in golden light as she sat at her dining table, a half-empty coffee cup beside her laptop.

She had an interview later that day, and curiosity had gotten the better of her. She typed "Angad Sareen" into the search bar.

Articles flooded the screen—business magazines, interviews, market analyses—but nothing personal. Mid-thirties. Graduated from a prestigious university in the US. No mention of a personal life. Just a few scattered images, mostly from corporate events.

Her eyes landed on one photo in particular. He stood at a gala, dressed in a crisp black suit, his expression unreadable. Even in the slightly pixelated image, his presence was undeniable. Tall—definitely over six feet. Sharp jawline, dark eyes, the kind of rugged handsomeness that seemed effortless. The kind that, she thought wryly, supermodel types would be drawn to.

Of course, men like him weren't single. Or if they were, it was by choice, a string of glamorous women at their disposal. She let out a small scoff at the thought. Men like him weren't for women like her. He looked like someone who belonged in a different world—one of power, luxury, and glamorous circles.

Reva, at 5'8", was tall for a woman—especially by Indian standards. She often towered over her peers, which made her self-conscious as a teenager and quietly apologetic as an adult. But height aside, she'd never thought of herself as particularly beautiful. Not in the magazine-cover, heads-turning, kind of way. She didn't have the chiseled cheekbones or the impossibly narrow waist that fashion editors seemed to worship.

Sure, she had the long legs—people told her that often enough—but she lacked the lean frame to match. She was, in her own words, "curvy"—a polite, functional term that women like her used in place of "bigger than ideal." Her hips had a natural curve to them—neither narrow nor overly wide, just soft, womanly, and real. Her thighs refused to shrink, and she had long ago made peace with the fact that no amount of Pilates or portion control would ever give her the runway look.

What she didn't know—or perhaps never fully believed—was how her presence filled a room. How her eyes lit up when she laughed, or how her warmth lingered long after she'd left. Because Reva had grown up learning to edit herself, to soften her brilliance and smooth out her edges. It had taken years—and heartbreaks—for her to stop apologizing for taking up space.

She shut her laptop, exhaling slowly. It didn't matter. She wasn't meeting him for anything other than work. Still, she couldn't shake the slight, nagging curiosity that lingered.

She had a long day ahead. An interview with Sareen Enterprise's digital news division awaited her, and though she had gone over every possible scenario in her head, she still felt a knot of unease in her stomach. This job could be a significant step in her career—a chance to work with a leading media house while still maintaining the flexibility she craved.

She wasn't one for rigid corporate structures, and she had made that clear in her initial discussions with the company's HR team. If they wanted her, it had to be on her terms. No nine-to-five confinements, no endless meetings just for the sake of them. She delivered results, and she did it best in her own space, at her own pace.

She knew the final call wouldn't come from HR, though. That decision rested with Angad Sareen. But today's meeting wasn't with him. It was just a formality with the team.

But before that, there was another commitment she couldn't push aside. She had to visit SLK International's junior branch for a review. As a board member, she made it a point to stay involved, ensuring the institution remained true to its core values despite its rapid expansion.

It was routine. Just another part of her structured life.

What she didn't know was that today, fate had other plans.

***

CHAPTER THREE

AN UNEXPECTED ENCOUNTER

The board meeting had taken longer than expected. It was already 12:30, and Reva was running late. She had the interview at 3 P.M. at Sareen Enterprises, and before that, she had a work deadline to meet. She hadn't had breakfast, and lunch seemed like a distant dream. The only thing keeping her going was coffee.

As she stepped out of the conference room, the kindergarten section of SLK International was abuzz with activity. The school day had ended for the little ones, and the corridors were filled with the sounds of excited chatter, the patter of tiny feet, and the occasional wail of a cranky child. She only intended to stop by the principal's office for a quick hello before rushing home to complete her pending work.

The universe, however, had its own script.

"Ree Di! Ree Di!"

She turned at the familiar call and saw her cousin Trisha, a teacher at the school, waving her over. Reva sighed, adjusting her tote bag on her shoulder. She could spare five minutes, she told herself.

As she spoke with her cousin, laughing over an old family joke, something out of the corner of her eye caught her attention. A little girl, no more than five years old, sat alone on a wooden bench in the play area, her tiny shoulders shaking.

Reva frowned and excused herself. The girl had a delicate face, a blend of Indian and Western features—hazel green eyes framed by dark lashes, soft brown curls, and a fair complexion with a hint of warmth. She looked different from the other children, her presence standing out. When she finally spoke, her voice carried a distinct American lilt.

Reva crouched down in front of the child, her voice soft. "Hey there, sweetheart. What's wrong?"

The girl looked up, her expressive eyes shimmering with unshed tears. She hiccupped. "Avik is mad at me."

Reva glanced around, trying to locate whoever Avik was.

Reva sat down beside her. "What happened? Why is he mad at you?"

The girl pouted. "I told Aarav and Zoya that he would play superheroes with them."

Reva suppressed a smile. "Oh? And he didn't like that?"

Anika shook her head so vigorously that her dark curls bounced around her face. "Nope! He said he doesn't want to."

Reva chuckled, amused by the fierce certainty in her voice. "Well, that does sound serious." She softened her tone. "And what's your name, sweetheart?"

"Anika," the little girl said.

Reva's smile widened. "That's a beautiful name, Anika." She paused, glancing around. "Now, tell me, where is this, Avik?"

The girl pointed toward the far corner. As Reva scanned the play area, her gaze landed on a little boy standing near the jungle gym, his arms tightly crossed over his chest, a deep frown etched onto his face. He looked like a miniature storm cloud, brooding and utterly unimpressed with the world around him. His tousled dark brown hair, slightly wavy, flopped over his forehead, and his sharp, almond-shaped eyes—so much like Anika's—were filled with unrelenting stubbornness.

Even at the age of five, there was something intense about him. He wasn't sulking like most kids his age would; he was simmering, his little jaw locked in frustration, his posture rigid with defiance. He wore a navy-blue polo shirt and beige shorts, both neatly pressed, but his shoes were slightly scuffed—maybe from a recent attempt at climbing the jungle gym.

Unlike Anika's soft, openly emotional demeanor, Avik had a certain quiet strength about him. He seemed like the type who didn't cry easily, who held onto his pride even when upset.

"That's Avik?" Reva asked.

The girl nodded. "Uh-huh. He's my brother."

Siblings, Reva thought fondly. They had the most dramatic fights over the silliest things.

She smiled gently. "Brothers can be silly sometimes. Want me to help?"

The little girl hesitated for a moment, then gave a small nod, rubbing her teary eyes with the back of her hand.

"He's my twin brother," Anika said as they started walking toward Avik.

Reva raised a brow, intrigued. "You're twins?"

Anika's face lit up with unmistakable pride. "Yes! But I was born first."

Reva smiled at her confidence and gently took her tiny hand. "Well then, big sister, let's go make things right."

When Reva approached, he barely spared her a glance, his little fists tightening. "She ruined everything," he muttered, his accent distinctly American, though his pronunciation had the occasional softness of someone who was beginning to pick up the rhythm of Indian speech.

Reva crouched beside him, curious now. "What did she do?"

Avik finally looked at her. His brow furrowed as though deciding whether she was worth talking to. "She told Aarav and Zoya that I would play superheroes with them. But I didn't want to play superheroes today. I wanted to play astronauts."

Reva bit back a smile at his serious tone. "And she didn't ask you first?"

"No." He kicked at a pebble near his foot, his frustration bubbling up. "She always decides stuff for me. Just 'cause she's older—by three minutes."

Reva glanced back at Anika, who was now watching them anxiously, her lower lip wobbling. "You know she didn't mean to upset you, right?"

Avik huffed but didn't respond, clearly still debating whether his sister was worth forgiving so quickly.

He glanced at his sister, who looked at him hopefully. With a reluctant sigh, he muttered, "Fine, I forgive you."

Anika's face lit up as she launched herself at him in a hug. Then, she turned back to Reva and grinned. "You're the best, Reedi!"

Reva blinked. "Reedi?"

"I heard Trisha Ma'am call you that," Anika explained. "So that's your name, right?"

Reva chuckled, ruffling the little girl's hair. "Close enough."

Reva crouched down to their level, her voice warm but curious. "So, who's coming to pick you up?"

Anika shrugged, still clutching Reva's hand as if she wasn't ready to let go just yet. "Lata Aunty. And Mohan Uncle, I think."

Reva tilted her head. "Mohan Uncle?"

"Our driver," Avik clarified, his tone making it clear that he found the explanation unnecessary.

Just as Reva was about to ask more, a frantic voice cut through the air. "There you are!"

They all turned to see a middle-aged woman rushing toward them, a man trailing behind her. The woman—Lata, Reva assumed—looked exasperated, her dupatta slipping off her shoulder as she hurried across the playground. The man beside her, likely Mohan, looked equally relieved.

"Why didn't you two come to the pick-up point?" Lata scolded, hands on her hips. "I've been looking everywhere! I even went to your classroom—" She huffed, cutting herself off as her gaze landed on Reva.

Reva quickly stood up, offering a small, reassuring smile. "I'm so sorry. It's my fault, really. I found Anika here, and she was upset. I didn't realize they were supposed to be somewhere."

Lata exhaled sharply, shaking her head. "These two, I tell you…"

Before she could say more, Anika suddenly hugged Reva around the waist. "Thank you, Reedi!"

Reva stiffened for a second before relaxing into the embrace.

"Reedi!" Avik echoed, grinning up at her before stepping forward to hug her, too—though he was quicker, almost reluctant, as if he didn't want to seem too affectionate.

Reva chuckled, gently ruffling Anika's curls. "You two are troublemakers, aren't you?"

The twins giggled, and Reva glanced at Lata, who still seemed flustered but less annoyed now.

"They're all yours," Reva said, stepping back. "I need to rush anyway. I have work to finish before heading out for an important meeting," she mumbled, more to herself than her audience.

Lata gave her a nod, still catching her breath, while Mohan motioned for the kids to follow.

As Reva walked away, she could still hear Anika's excited voice chattering in the background.

"Reedi is nice, right, Avik?"

Reva smiled to herself as she exited the school grounds. She had a long evening ahead—deadlines to meet and then, of course, the interview at Sareen Enterprises.

Little did she know, her life had already begun to change in ways she hadn't imagined.

***

CHAPTER FOUR

THE FIRST MEETING

Reva barely had time to breathe as she rushed home from SLK International. The moment she stepped into her apartment, she tossed her bag onto the couch and headed straight to her bedroom. She needed to change, grab her laptop, and be out the door in less than twenty minutes.

Shrugging off her kurta, she pulled out an elegant yet professional navy-blue sheath dress from her closet. Simple, structured, and formal enough for an interview. She quickly ran a brush through her hair, pulling it into a sleek, low ponytail, then slipped on a pair of nude pumps. A swipe of nude lipstick, a final glance in the mirror, and she was ready.

Grabbing her laptop bag, she hurried out the door, making a mental note to eat something later. Her stomach grumbled in protest, but there was no time.

By some miracle, traffic wasn't as bad as she had feared, and she reached Sareen Enterprises with a few minutes to spare.

The towering glass building radiated power and prestige, exactly as she had expected. Taking a steadying breath, Reva adjusted her bag on her shoulder and stepped inside. The lobby was a study in modern elegance—polished marble floors gleamed under recessed lighting, and a massive digital screen near the entrance cycled through the latest headlines from Sareen Media's various platforms. Sareen Enterprises occupied the 17th and 18th floors, its top two levels, exclusively.

She made her way to the reception desk, her heels clicking against the floor. "Reva Khanna. I have a 3 P.M. interview with Nishant Sharma from Sareen Enterprises," she said with practiced professionalism.

The receptionist smiled. “Yes, ma’am. Take the elevator to the 18th floor. Mr. Sharma will meet you there.”

Reva nodded, murmuring her thanks before making her way to the elevator. As she ascended, she squared her shoulders and reminded herself why she was here. This was just another meeting, another professional engagement. It didn’t matter that Sareen Enterprises was one of the biggest names in the media or that its CEO was a man who looked more like a rugged movie star than a business tycoon. It didn’t matter that she had Googled him earlier, finding nothing but carefully curated articles and images. Even Google yielded nothing Angad hadn’t approved for the world to see—this was exactly what you’d expect from a media mogul.

None of that mattered. She was here for work. That was it.

Nishant Sharma, a pleasant-looking man in his mid-30s, greeted her in the conference room with a firm handshake. “Ms. Khanna, a pleasure to finally meet you in person. I’ve gone through your portfolio, and I must say, it’s impressive.”

“Thank you,” Reva replied, settling into a chair across from him.

They spent the next thirty minutes discussing the role, the expectations, and the contract terms. Nishant was professional and direct, and she appreciated that. When they reached the discussion about her working conditions, he hesitated slightly.

“You’re quite firm on the flexibility aspect,” he noted. “Most people at your level prefer a more structured role.”

Reva smiled, prepared for this question. “I produce my best work when I’m not bound by rigid hours. And my track record speaks for itself.”

Nishant chuckled. “Fair enough.” He glanced at his phone before looking back at her. “Mr. Sareen would like to have a word with you before we proceed further. Do you have some time?”

Reva stiffened slightly; she wasn’t supposed to meet him today. Her belly voiced its discontent, but she ignored it. “Of course.”

*

Angad Sareen was not having a good day.

Meetings had run over schedule, his kids had given Lata a hard time, and on top of that, his editorial team was still not aligned with the vision he had for their upcoming online news portal. He needed this to be perfect. He didn’t do half-measures.

And that’s where Reva Khanna came in.

Her name had stuck in his mind since he first saw her file.

He had done his research. An MBA in digital media from a reputed university in the US, one of the most sought-after freelance consultants in the country, a woman who dictated her own terms and refused to conform to traditional work setups. That last bit had annoyed him at first.

He wasn't used to people dictating conditions in his own company. And yet, he had agreed.

Now, he needed to see if she was truly as good as everyone claimed her to be.

Nishant led Reva into the expansive corner office, where floor-to-ceiling windows offered a sweeping view of Gurugram's ever-growing skyline. The room was sharp and modern—glass, steel, and dark wood blending into an atmosphere of quiet power. At the center of it all stood Angad Sareen.

He was even more striking in person than in the few pictures she had found online. Tall—easily six feet two—broad-shouldered, dressed in a crisp white shirt with the sleeves rolled up just enough to hint at strong forearms. His beard was neatly trimmed, lending a rugged edge to his otherwise sophisticated presence. A man used to control. Command.

Reva wasn't easily intimidated, but something about him made her straighten her spine.

Angad, meanwhile, also observed the woman standing before him. She was tall—maybe 5'7" or 5'8" without her heels, if he had to guess—her curvy frame carried an air of quiet confidence. She wasn't the type of woman he usually saw in high-profile media circles, where glamour often outshone substance. But there was something refreshingly real about her—thick, dark hair pulled into a low ponytail, minimal makeup, sharp eyes that didn't shy away from his gaze.

"This is Reva Khanna," Nishant said, breaking the silence. "One of the best digital media consultants in the country." He turned to her. "And this, of course, is Angad Sareen, our CEO."

Angad extended a hand, and Reva hesitated for just a second before slipping hers into his. His grip was firm, warm, but not overbearing. A simple handshake, yet something about it made the air shift.

Her pulse jumped—unexpectedly. He held her gaze a second longer than necessary, his dark eyes studying her as if peeling back layers.

"Ms. Khanna." His voice was deep, steady.

"Mr. Sareen," she returned, her own voice smooth despite the strange flutter in her chest.

Nishant, oblivious to the unspoken tension, smiled. "I'll leave you both to discuss the role further. I'll check in later." With that, he stepped out, leaving them alone.

For a beat, the silence stretched between them.

"Please, have a seat," Angad said finally, gesturing toward the chair opposite his desk.

She sat, crossing one leg over the other, trying to shake off the remnants of whatever that handshake had been.

Angad leaned back slightly, studying her as if trying to reconcile the woman before him with the one he had read about in countless work portfolios. She didn't fit into any of the easy categories.

"So, Ms. Khanna," he said, steepling his fingers, "your work speaks for itself. But I'll be honest—I wasn't expecting someone with your background to insist on a flexible schedule. Most professionals looking to climb higher want stability and structure."

Reva met his gaze without hesitation. "With all due respect, Mr. Sareen, I'm not looking to climb anywhere. I prefer to work on my own terms, and that flexibility is what allows me to deliver my best. The work matters to me, not the hours I clock in."

He watched her closely, his expression shifting just for a moment—too brief to catch. "And what is it about this particular role that interests you?"

She hesitated, then answered honestly. "Digital media is the present and the future, and from what I've read, Sareen Enterprises wants to be ahead of the curve. That's the kind of project I want to be part of."

He nodded slightly as if satisfied with the answer.

The conversation stretched on, discussing content strategies, audience engagement, and editorial direction. Angad was intense and razor-sharp, and he had a vision she could respect. Reva found herself drawn in despite herself.

But just as their discussion reached a lull, an unmistakable sound filled the quiet office.

A loud stomach grumble.

Reva froze.

Oh no.

Angad arched an eyebrow.

Heat rushed to her cheeks. She hadn't eaten all day—hadn't even realized how empty her stomach was until now. It was already 4.30 in the evening.

"That," she muttered, straightening, "was embarrassing."

A smirk threatened at the corner of his mouth—the first real crack in his composure since she'd entered.

"I'd offer you a business contract," he said, deadpan, "but perhaps you'd prefer a sandwich first?"

She exhaled a short laugh, shaking her head. "I'll survive, but thank you."

He leaned back, watching her for a moment. "Are you sure? I have a standing lunch order. I can get something sent in."

She hesitated—because the thought of food was tempting—but shook her head. "I appreciate it, really. But I should go."

Angad gave a slow nod. "Very well. Expect an official email from HR soon."

She stood, smoothing her dress, and he rose too. Their eyes met again, and for a moment, neither moved.

"Thank you for your time, Mr. Sareen."

He didn't immediately respond. When he spoke, his tone was steady, but his eyes hinted at something else. "Welcome to Sareen Enterprises, Ms. Khanna."

As she turned to leave, she could still feel the weight of his gaze on her back.

***

CHAPTER FIVE

STOMACH SATIATION

As Reva walked out of Angad's office, her cheeks still heated from the embarrassing stomach grumble, Angad leaned back in his chair, exhaling deeply.

What the hell was that?

Reva Khanna.

He had done his research. She was sharp, confident, and highly sought after in the industry. But nothing in those reports had prepared him for the reality of her—the way she carried herself, the way she spoke with such clarity, and the way she challenged him without a hint of intimidation.

And then there was the stomach grumble—so human, so real, completely shattering the composed image she projected. It should've been funny. It *was* funny. But it had also been oddly endearing.

And that was the problem.

Angad didn't do attraction at work. He didn't get distracted. He had too much at stake—his children, his business. And yet, something about her tugged at him.

He rubbed his jaw, frustrated. *What the fuck, Sareen?*

With a shake of his head, Angad shut his laptop and leaned back in his chair, exhaling slowly. There was still work to be done—there always was—but it could wait until later. He pressed his fingers to his temples, trying to ease the tension, before glancing at his phone. It was later than he had intended, but he had promised himself he would get home early today.

Except, before heading home, there was one more stop to make.

Anika and Avik had been going on and on about chocolate pastries for days now, dropping not-so-subtle hints at every opportunity. He had meant to pick them up yesterday but was caught up in back-to-back meetings. Today, there were no excuses.

Pushing back his chair, he grabbed his phone and slipped on his jacket. The café downstairs had the best selection—rich, decadent pastries that would light up the twins' faces the moment they saw them.

That thought alone made the detour worth it.

As he stepped into the elevator, his thoughts drifted back to Reva—her handshake, the way she held his gaze, unflinching and confident. There was something about her presence that unsettled him in a way he hadn't expected. She wasn't the kind of woman who turned heads the moment she walked into a room—no, her appeal was more subtle, more insidious. It crept up on him, catching him off guard when he least expected it.

She wasn't slender like the women he usually found himself surrounded by—models, socialites, women who thrived in his world of power and influence. No, she had fair skin with a warm undertone, sharp eyes that didn't waver, and those curves—*God*, those curves.

She was soft in all the right places, her body made for indulgence, for slow exploration. The thought came unbidden, unwanted, yet there it was, searing itself into his mind.

And her mouth. Damn, that mouth. Full, expressive, the kind that could make a man forget his own name if she whispered it just right. He imagined what it would feel like to taste her, to have those lips part beneath his, to hear the way her breath would hitch—

He cut off that thought immediately. *No. Not happening.*

He was not some reckless teenager losing his mind over a woman he had just met. He was disciplined and controlled. Besides, they were going to be working together. And he wasn't looking for a fling—especially not with someone he would have to see regularly. He had too much at stake, too many responsibilities.

Yet, as the elevator doors slid open, he exhaled sharply, running a hand over his jaw.

This was going to be a problem.

*

Reva left Angad's office with her heart still hammering, her cheeks burning with embarrassment. Of all the things that could have happened, her stomach had to betray her at the most mortifying moment.

What must he think of her?

Probably that, she was some starved, ill-mannered woman who didn't even have the sense to eat before a meeting. Groaning internally, Reva practically fled to the café on the ground floor. She needed food—lots of food. *Desperately.*

The cafe on the ground floor of the Sareen Enterprises building was buzzing with activity, but she managed to slide into a small table in the corner. She placed her order: a strong cappuccino, a grilled chicken sandwich, and, because she absolutely deserved it after the day she had had—cheesecake.

As she took her first bite, she let out an involuntary sigh of relief. Finally, food.

Her mind, however, refused to cooperate, keeping her thoughts drifting back to Angad Sareen. His voice, deep and smooth, still echoed in her ears. He was... intriguing. Intimidating. But also, magnetic. And then, there was the way he looked at her. Observant, assessing, but not unkind.

And that handshake—

Her fingers twitched slightly at the memory. She had shaken hands with hundreds of people, but this... this had been different. A slow burn of awareness, a tingle up her arm.

His handshake had sent a surprising jolt through her body, one she hadn't expected. It had been firm, warm, and lingering—almost as if he, too, had felt something.

She swallowed hard. *If a handshake felt like that... what would a kiss feel like?*

The thought came uninvited, and before she could stop herself, her mind conjured an image—his dark eyes, his firm lips pressing against hers, the way his rough stubble would feel against her skin—

She squeezed her eyes shut. *No, no, no! Stop that right now, Reva!*

A deep voice interrupted her thoughts.

"Daydreaming about something, Ms. Khanna?"

Her eyes flew open, and she nearly choked on her coffee.

Angad Sareen stood before her, smirking.

Oh, hell.

Her face burned as she quickly composed herself, reaching for her napkin as if that could somehow erase her mortification. "Mr. Sareen," she greeted, trying to sound unaffected. "What a surprise."

His lips twitched slightly as if he knew exactly how flustered she was. "May I join you?"

No, you absolutely may not, her brain screamed. But her mouth had other plans. "Of course."

As he settled into the seat across from her, a waiter approached, setting a neatly packed paper bag in front of him. "Your order, sir. Chocolate éclairs and fruit pastries, as requested."

Angad nodded in acknowledgment, then glanced at Reva's plate. "Good cheesecake?" he asked casually.

She straightened slightly, taken aback. "Uh… yeah. It's good."

Without missing a beat, he turned to the waiter. "An Americano. And a cheesecake."

Reva arched a brow. "Didn't peg you for a cheesecake guy."

Angad smirked, then gestured toward her nearly empty plate. "You want something else?"

She shook her head. "I'm good."

"You sure?" His tone was casual, but there was something in the way he asked, like he was making an effort to keep the conversation going.

Reva gave him a small smile. "Positive."

He shrugged, leaning back in his chair. "Nothing like coffee and cheesecake to take a break."

Her pulse skittered, but she masked it with a casual smile. "So, you don't usually take breaks?"

"Not really. But sometimes, a change of scenery helps." His gaze flicked to her, lingering just a second too long before he looked away. "And you? Always work through lunch?"

She let out a small laugh. "Not intentionally. Today was just hectic. Meetings, deadlines… and, of course, my stomach decided to make itself known in your office."

Angad chuckled, a deep, rich sound that sent a shiver down her spine. "It was a first, I'll admit. But at least now I know you have good taste in desserts."

Reva smiled, her embarrassment fading. He was easy to talk to—more so than she'd expected. For a man who exuded power and control, he wasn't cold or distant.

As they continued their small talk, Angad's phone rang. He glanced at the caller ID, a softer expression crossed his face as he answered.

"Yes, my love?" His voice lowered slightly, the warmth in it unmistakable. "I've got it. Yes, sweetheart, I'll be home soon."

Reva's stomach twisted unexpectedly. She took a sip of her coffee, focusing on anything but the pang of disappointment that hit her. Of course, a man like Angad Sareen wouldn't be single. He probably had a stunning girlfriend—or a wife—waiting for him at home. Someone effortlessly elegant, maybe a supermodel or a businesswoman just as successful as he is.

He hung up, slipping the phone back into his pocket, and turned back to her. "Sorry about that."

"No problem," she said lightly, hoping she sounded unaffected.

A few beats of silence stretched between them before he gestured toward her now-empty plate. "Satisfied?"

"For now." She smirked. "I should probably get going."

He nodded, though not without a moment's pause. "It was… nice running into you."

She tilted her head. "Was it?"

Angad let out a low chuckle. For a split second, something stirred in his eyes, elusive and unspoken. "Yes, Ms Khanna. It was."

Before she could respond, he signaled for the bill. When it arrived, he pulled out his card before she could even reach for her purse.

She frowned. "You didn't have to—"

"I know," he cut in smoothly.

Reva exhaled, shaking her head. "Then next time, it'll be on me."

Angad slid his wallet back into his pocket, a trace of amusement tugging at his lips. "So, there will be a next time?"

Her breath hitched slightly, but she masked it with a quick, almost flippant response. "Well… now that we'll be working together… who knows?"

As she stood, their eyes met once more. And in that brief moment, something passed between them—something undeniable.

With one last glance, she gathered her things and left. As she walked away, she could still feel his gaze on her back. And despite everything, she couldn't help but wonder if she'd just stepped into something far more complicated than she had anticipated.

***

CHAPTER SIX

FRIENDSHIP

Reva had been looking forward to spending the evening with her niece, Sanaya. The six-year-old was a whirlwind of energy, a constant chatterbox, and the light of Reva's life. Her excitement was infectious, and despite the exhaustion from back-to-back meetings, Reva had promised her an ice cream date—just the two of them.

Sanaya was her sister's daughter, lived in Mumbai, and had come to stay with their parents for a few days while both her parents were traveling. Technically, she was staying at her grandparents' place, but in reality, she was practically glued to Reva, following her around like a shadow.

"My favorite person in the whole world," she often declared, her little arms flung around Reva's waist. And though Reva had never considered herself particularly maternal, she had to admit—if she ever had a daughter, she'd want one exactly like Sanaya.

However, Sanaya had her own plans. "*Maasi*, let's go to the clubhouse!" she had insisted, eyes wide with excitement.

"You don't want ice cream?" Reva had teased, arching a brow.

"We can get ice cream later," Sanaya had declared with a dramatic wave of her hand. "I want to go play!"

And that was how they ended up at the clubhouse of their society, a lively hub of children running around, shrieking with laughter, and parents or nannies keeping a watchful eye. The air was filled with the mingling scents of fresh grass and chlorine from the pool, the hum of conversations blending with the occasional call of a parent reminding a child not to run.

Sanaya wasted no time. The moment they stepped in, she spotted a group of kids she recognized and ran toward them, her tiny feet barely touching the ground.

Reva smiled, shaking her head as she settled onto one of the lounge chairs nearby. It was a scene she had grown familiar with—Sanaya effortlessly making friends, her boundless enthusiasm drawing children in like a magnet.

She pulled out her phone, intending to catch up on some unread emails while keeping an eye on Sanaya. As Reva sank into a corner seat, her mind, yet again, wandered to Angad—just as it had been doing for days now, more specifically, to the pastries he had ordered the other day. For his girlfriend or wife, she wondered. The thought irked her more than it should. She imagined him sharing the pastry with a stunning, model-like woman, both of them laughing over coffee. The jealousy that twisted inside her was unsettling. *What was wrong with her?*

Her spiraling thoughts snapped back to reality when she heard a high-pitched whine.

"But I want a chocolate eclair!" a little girl demanded, stomping her tiny foot.

Reva turned, surprised to see the familiar face of Anika from the school. The girl was standing near the clubhouse snack counter, glaring at the woman next to her, Lata Aunty.

"No, Anika baby," Lata said firmly. "You've already had your treat for the week. Your daddy wouldn't like it."

Reva smiled and walked over. "Anika, hi there. Remember me?"

Anika's teary eyes widened. "Reedi!"

Avik appeared at her side, frowning. "What are you doing here?"

"I live here," Reva said, amused. "And guess what? I'm here with my niece, Sanaya. She's right there. Would you like to be friends with her?"

At the mention of a new friend, Anika perked up immediately. "She lives here, too?"

"She's here for a few days," Reva confirmed. "Why don't you go say 'hi' while I sort this chocolate problem?"

Anika ran to Sanaya while Avik trailed behind, looking more cautious. Reva turned to Lata, who looked uneasy.

"I hope it's alright if I get them something?"

Lata hesitated. "Sir wouldn't—"

"It's just a treat. Kids should get to be kids," Reva said, then ordered three chocolate eclairs.

When the pastries arrived, the children cheered, instantly bonding over their shared love for chocolate. Within minutes, Sanaya had invited Anika and Avik over to 'Maasi's house' the next evening to play.

*

Later that evening, back at home, the twins were practically bouncing with excitement as they narrated their evening to Angad.

"And Reedi bought us chocolate eclairs!" Anika beamed.

"Yeah, and she lives here! In our complex!" Avik added.

Angad's brows snapped together. "Who is Reedi?"

"I think her name is Riddhi. She was talking to them at school, too," Lata supplied hesitantly. "She helped them sort out a small fight."

His frown deepened. "You're telling me a woman we don't know—a stranger, whose name you're only guessing—has spoken to my children not once, but twice? First at school, and now again at the clubhouse? And she gave them food?"

Lata winced, "She seems to come from a good family. She was just being nice."

"That's not the point," Angad snapped, his protectiveness kicking in. "And how do you know she's from a good family? Do you know her family?" He turned to the kids. "You don't accept food from strangers. And you don't talk to strangers. Do you understand me?"

The twins shrank under his hard gaze. "Yes, Daddy."

He ran a hand through his hair, frustration simmering. This couldn't be a coincidence. Who was this woman? And why was she interacting with his kids?

"I need to talk to the school," he muttered. "How could they let a stranger talk to my kids?"

*

The next morning, Angad exhaled sharply as he drove towards SLK International, his grip tightening on the steering wheel. His patience was already worn thin from the morning rush, and now this. How could the school allow a stranger to interact with his kids? His kids. His responsibility.

The sleek glass entrance of SLK International gleamed under the late morning sun as he pulled up in front of the security gate. The guard barely had time to nod before Angad strode past, his long strides eating up the distance to the administrative wing.

Inside, the air was crisp, tinged with the faint scent of polished wood and fresh paper. A young woman at the front desk looked up, momentarily startled by his imposing presence. She quickly rose to her feet, smoothing her uniform.

"Good afternoon, Mr. Sareen. How can I help you?"

"I need to speak with the principal. Right now," Angad stated, his voice even but firm.

The woman hesitated, eyes darting toward the schedule on her screen. "Mrs. Ahuja is in a meeting, but—"

"Then get her out of it," he interrupted smoothly. "This is a security concern regarding my children."

That did the trick. Within moments, he was being led down the corridor toward the principal's office.

*

Meera Ahuja looked up as Angad strode in, her sharp eyes assessing him in a heartbeat. She had dealt with her fair share of difficult parents, but there was an unmistakable intensity about this man.

"Mr. Sareen," she greeted professionally, gesturing for him to take a seat. "I understand you have concerns?"

Angad remained standing. "There's been a security lapse, Mrs. Ahuja. I only found out yesterday that a woman—a stranger—who approached my children in our residential complex last evening, also interacted with them during school hours a few days ago. How was this allowed to happen? Where was the security then?"

Meera's brow furrowed slightly, but her voice remained composed. "I assure you, we take security very seriously at SLK International. If you could give me more details, I will personally look into the matter."

"Her name is Riddhi. Or at least, that's what she told the kids," Angad said, jaw clenching. "I want to know how she got access to them. This is unacceptable."

Meera's frown deepened. "Riddhi?" she repeated, clearly at a loss. "I don't believe we have anyone by that name associated with the school. Are you certain she wasn't another parent? A guardian?"

Angad's frustration flared. "I don't know who she is! That's the point. And I expect the school to find out. How could you allow an unidentified woman to talk to my children? Do you have any idea how dangerous that could be?"

Meera held his gaze steadily. "Mr. Sareen, I understand your concern, but before I escalate this matter, I need to know—what exactly did this woman say to your children?"

That made him pause. What had she said? He had been so consumed with the fact that a stranger had interacted with them that he hadn't even asked about the actual conversation.

Meera tilted her head. "Did she threaten them? Did she try to take them somewhere? Offer them anything suspicious?"

Angad's silence stretched between them before he finally ground out, "I'll ask them. But I expect a report on this. And if I don't get satisfactory answers, I will escalate this to the school board."

She nodded. "Understood. But Sir, Mr. Sareen, if there was no security breach, then perhaps this isn't a case of negligence, but a misunderstanding."

Angad exhaled sharply. He had come in expecting immediate action, maybe even a security overhaul, not calm reasoning.

Meera studied him for a moment before saying, "I understand you're protective of your children. It's commendable. But I also believe a parent's instinct should be balanced with understanding. Let me know what your children tell you, and if anything concerning comes up, we will address it. Meanwhile, we'll review our security tapes."

He didn't like it. But he also knew she wasn't wrong. With a curt nod, he left.

*

By the time Angad reached home later that evening, he was still simmering with frustration. He found Anika and Avik curled up on the couch, watching cartoons.

"Pause that for a minute," he instructed. They obeyed, turning to him with identical curious expressions.

He sat down across from them, voice firm but calm. "Tell me exactly what happened with this—Riddhi. What did she say to you at school?"

Anika launched into an animated retelling of how *Reedi* had helped her resolve her fight with Avik at school. "She was super nice, Daddy! And she made Avik talk to me again. She said brothers and sisters fight, but we still love each other."

Angad shifted his gaze to his son. "And you? What do you think?"

Avik hesitated, then shrugged. "She wasn't bad."

That wasn't the ringing endorsement Anika gave, but it wasn't damning either.

Angad's jaw tightened. "And at the clubhouse?"

Avik answered this time. "Anika was throwing a tantrum about the chocolate pastry, and Sanaya and Reedi bought it for us. That's all, Daddy."

"Sanaya?"

"Her niece, Daddy," Anika chimed in. "She's a year older than us, and she invited us to her apartment to play." She grinned, clearly excited.

"Hmm," Angad pinched the bridge of his nose. He had stormed into the school demanding answers, and the woman—whoever she was—had simply… helped the kids?

Was he overreacting? His protectiveness over the kids often made him wary, but had he been too hasty in assuming the worst?

He exhaled, his gaze softening as he looked at them. "Listen to me, both of you. We do not take anything from strangers. No matter how sweet they seem. Do you understand?"

Anika frowned. "But we met her twice, and she lives here. How is she a stranger?"

Angad's expression turned steely. "She's a stranger until Daddy says so."

If this woman had any intentions—good or bad—he needed to know. And he would find out.

Soon.

*

The next evening at the clubhouse, Angad took extra precautions. Along with Lata, he sent Mohan, making it clear that they were to keep a close watch on the kids.

When Reva arrived at the clubhouse with Sanaya and waved at the twins, she immediately sensed the shift in the air.

Lata tensed the moment she spotted her, her grip tightening around Anika and Avik's hands as if preparing to leave.

"What's going on?" Reva asked, frowning.

The twins exchanged nervous glances before Anika mumbled, "Daddy said we can't talk to you."

Reva blinked. "What?"

Avik, looking equally guilty and hesitant, added, "And we can't eat anything you give us… because you're a stranger."

A sharp sting of irritation pricked at Reva's temper. "A stranger?" she repeated, incredulous. She turned to Lata. "Did he seriously say that?"

Lata shifted uncomfortably but didn't confirm or deny it. Her silence was answer enough.

Reva exhaled through her nose, trying to keep her voice even. "Fine. If he's so concerned, why isn't he here himself? Why isn't their mother here with them? Why leave them with a nanny?"

She regretted the words the moment she caught the hurt in Lata's eyes.

Before Lata could say anything, Avik spoke up, his little face scrunched in frustration. "We don't have a mother," he said, his voice wobbling slightly but firm. "Daddy loves us a lot. But he also has a lot of work."

Reva's breath hitched. The sharp retort she had been about to fire off died on her lips.

For a moment, she just looked at Avik, then at Anika, whose lower lip trembled slightly.

Guilt twisted inside her.

She had been so focused on the insult—on the idea that she had been branded as a 'stranger'—that she hadn't considered the reason behind their father's–correction, *their single father's*–overprotectiveness.

She glanced at Sanaya. If someone gave her food and talked to her, and she didn't know them well enough, wouldn't Reva be concerned, too?

Damn it.

She swallowed, forcing herself to soften. "I didn't mean…" She sighed, rubbing her temple before looking at Lata. "I'm sorry. That wasn't fair of me."

Lata still looked hesitant, but she gave a small nod.

Reva crouched down to the twins' level. "I understand why your dad is being careful. He just wants to keep you safe."

Anika's little brow furrowed. "But we've met you three times now. And you live here. How are you a stranger?"

Reva almost smiled, but Avik beat her to responding. "Daddy says… you're a stranger until he says so."

Reva pressed her lips together. That overbearing, arrogant…

She shook her head. "Alright, then. You listen to your daddy, okay?"

Anika and Avik nodded, though they looked a little sad.

Reva turned to Lata, her voice measured but firm. "Tell their father that I live in this complex—Apartment 309. If he has a problem, he's welcome to come and speak to me directly."

She took a breath, reigning in her frustration before continuing, "And while you're at it, let him know that Avik and Anika are always welcome to play with Sanaya—whether here at the clubhouse or my apartment. The kids shouldn't be punished for something that isn't their fault."

Her gaze darted to the twins, who stood quietly beside Lata, their expressions uncertain. Softening her tone just a fraction, she added, "If he has any concerns, he's more than welcome to drop them off himself. I have nothing to hide."

Without waiting for a response, she took Sanaya's hand and turned to leave, ignoring the tug of guilt gnawing at her chest. Behind her, she heard Anika's small, heartbroken voice.

"But I wanted to play with Sanaya..."

Sanaya tugged at Reva's hand, her little face creased with worry. "Maasi, I want to play with them too."

Reva swallowed, her jaw tightening. This wasn't fair—to the kids, to anyone. But if their father wanted to pick a battle over something so trivial, then fine. He could come to her.

Her heart ached for the twins. They didn't have a mother. And their father... he was overprotective, overbearing, and clearly didn't trust easily.

Whoever their father was, he seemed hell-bent on controlling everything around them. And for some reason, that fact irked her more than it should.

***

CHAPTER SEVEN

PUSH AND PULL

Reva stepped into Sareen Enterprise's sleek, expansive office, the hum of quiet efficiency settling around her like a familiar rhythm. She had been here before, but this was the first time she was meeting the design team in person.

Her gaze swept across the workspace—rows of focused employees, the occasional sound of fingers tapping briskly against keyboards, muted conversations blending into the background. Then, her eyes found the glass-walled cabin at the far side of the floor.

Angad Sareen.

Even through the glass, his presence was commanding. He stood tall, shoulders squared, engaged in a phone call. There was something effortlessly authoritative about him—the way he held himself, the way his fingers drummed absently against the desk as he listened, the sharp, assessing glint in his gaze when he finally turned.

And found her.

Their eyes met through the glass, a flicker of something indecipherable passing between them. His lips lifted—not a smile exactly, but something edged with amusement, almost too knowing. He murmured a few final words into the phone before hanging up. As she approached his cabin, he stepped out, leaning casually against the doorway, arms folded across his chest.

"I was beginning to think you'd run away," he drawled.

Reva arched a brow, unfazed. "From what? A meeting?"

"From me."

She rolled her eyes but couldn't ignore the slight dip in her stomach at the way he said it—low, teasing, self-assured. Instead of dignifying it with a response, she brushed past him, heading towards the conference room.

Behind her, she heard him chuckle softly. "Have you had anything to eat?"

Reva hesitated mid-step, then turned back to face him. She'd grabbed a quick coffee before leaving home, but food? Not quite. She was about to deflect when his gaze sharpened.

"I was… working," she admitted, deciding to be honest. She had a feeling he'd see through her if she said anything else but the truth.

Angad's expression didn't change, but a glint of amusement flashed in his eyes—sharp, subtle, and impossible to ignore. "Multitasking is great, Ms. Khanna, but eating is non-negotiable." His voice had dropped just a fraction, the smooth cadence settling over her skin like an unexpected jolt.

Before she could argue, he turned to his assistant. "Get me some sandwiches and coffee from the café downstairs. Cappuccino for Ms. Khanna. She will be joining me."

"I—"

"No arguments." His tone was firm yet deceptively light, a mix of command and casual charm.

She hesitated. But fine—she *was* hungry. And maybe, just maybe, a small part of her was curious about what lunch with Angad Sareen would be like.

Inside his office, the space was as striking as the man himself. Floor-to-ceiling windows framed the city skyline, a sleek wooden desk dominated one side, and a rich leather couch sat near a low coffee table. Everything was curated and controlled, yet still inviting.

He gestured toward the seating area near the windows. "Sit."

"Thank you, Mr. Sareen," she said, lowering herself onto the couch.

Then, with a slow smirk, he added, "Angad. Please call me Angad, Reva."

She hated how her name sounded, almost… indulgent when he said it. She ignored the thought.

He sat across from her, resting an arm along the back of the couch, his gaze sharp and impossible to read. "I won't have you passing out in the middle of a meeting or, worse, letting everyone hear your stomach growl in the conference room." His lips curved, his voice dropping into something smooth and suggestive. "Let some sounds remain private... between us."

Reva froze.

The words slid between playful and provocative, setting off a flurry of confusion in her mind. Was he... flirting? No, that couldn't be right. He didn't seem the type. And he certainly wasn't available.

Not when he had someone back home—a girlfriend, a wife, whoever it was—that he bought pastries for.

A ridiculous pang of jealousy struck before she could stop it. Why did she care if he had a picture-perfect domestic life waiting for him?

She scoffed, lifting her chin. "Wow. That's a whole new level of concern for my well-being, Mr. Sareen."

"Angad." He corrected her.

"Angad." She said.

His smirk deepened as he studied her. His eyes lingered on her, a brief shadow crossing his expression. The way his name rolled off her tongue, smooth yet laced with challenge, sent a sharp jolt through him. He shouldn't care. It was just a name. But damn if it didn't sound different coming from her—like a dare, like a promise, like something he suddenly wanted to hear again.

What the fuck was he thinking? And what the hell was he saying to her?

This wasn't him. He didn't flirt at work. He didn't flirt, period. But something about her—the way she held herself, the way she pushed back against him—unsettled his usual restraint. It was irritating. It was intriguing.

And it needed to stop.

"Call it an act of self-preservation," he said smoothly, recovering. "I'd rather not deal with a consultant fainting in the middle of a heated debate over font choices."

Reva exhaled, forcing herself to relax. Whatever that moment was, she was reading too much into it.

A few minutes later, his assistant brought in their order: a tray with fresh fruit, sandwiches, and croissants, a black coffee for him and a cappuccino for her.

"You just assumed my order?" she asked, one brow lifting.

"I pay attention." His voice was smooth, matter-of-fact. "I know you like cappuccino and sandwiches, and you seem like a croissant kind of woman."

Reva picked up the flaky pastry and bit into it. Damn him. It was perfect.

He leaned back in his chair, watching her. "So, how's my design team treating you?"

"We're getting there," she said between bites. "The framework is solid, but there are some structural changes I want to discuss."

Angad smirked. "I had a feeling you'd say that."

After they finished eating, they moved to the boardroom, where the meeting quickly turned heated.

The discussion about the website's structure and user interface turned into a battle of wills. Angad, with his sharp business acumen and years of experience, had a firm vision. Reva, with her expertise in content presentation, argued for a more reader-friendly design.

"This layout is too text-heavy," Reva pointed out, gesturing to the mockup.

"That's because it's a news portal, not a fashion blog," Angad shot back.

"You can have content without making it look cluttered."

"And you can have aesthetics without compromising information."

"That layout will make navigation clunky," she argued.

"And your version slows down the page," he countered, arms crossed.

Reva huffed, glaring at him. "User experience matters more than—"

"Functionality is key," he interrupted, voice calm but firm. "We're not just making it pretty, Reva. We're making it work."

The tension between them charged the air, sharp and crackling. Neither of them backed down easily, their voices rising slightly with each counterpoint.

The team sat in silence, watching them like spectators at a tennis match.

Reva's jaw was tight; her fingers curled into fists on the table. Angad, on the other hand, was maddeningly composed, his expression neutral except for the glint of challenge in his eyes.

"Look, you brought me in for my expertise," she said finally, exasperated. "Let me do my job."

Angad leaned back, studying her. Then, to her surprise, he smirked. "Alright. I'll let you have this one."

She narrowed her eyes. "You *let* me?"

"I pick my battles, Reva." He closed his laptop. "And I'd like to see you win."

Her breath caught for half a second before she forced herself to look away. Infuriating man.

*

It had been a busy week. Reva wrapped up her last meeting of the evening, feeling the weight of the day settle over her. It was productive—she had finalized edits for another client's project, checked a few things off her never-ending to-do list, and was now finally heading home.

Yet, despite the mental satisfaction of completing her tasks, a persistent thought clung to her mind. Or rather, a persistent man.

Angad Sareen.

Even after a few days, she was still thinking about their last meeting, still replaying that damn conversation in her head. The heated debate, the verbal sparring, the sharp glint in his eyes as they went toe-to-toe. And then, when she thought they would keep arguing into eternity, he had relented. Just like that. But not before throwing out that infuriatingly smooth, almost indulgent, "*I'd like to see you win.*"

What was that supposed to mean?

She sighed, leaning back against the car seat as the city lights blurred past. She needed to stop overanalyzing. Angad was a frustrating, insufferable man, and this was just work. Nothing more.

Her phone buzzed.

She glanced at the screen, expecting a message from her mother asking when she was reaching home. Instead, it was him.

Angad Sareen: *Urgent website meeting. 6:30 PM. My place.*

Reva frowned, hesitating.

Reva Khanna: *Can't this wait until tomorrow?*

It was beyond office hours, and she wasn't about to let Angad dictate her schedule just because he decided something was "urgent."

Angad Sareen: *No.*

Her fingers hovered over the phone screen, irritation bubbling up. The absolute arrogance of the man. She was about to type out a firm '**Not happening.**' when another message popped up—his address and location pin.

Her brows lifted as she clicked on it.

He lived in her society. The building across from hers. And, of course, it had to be the 15th floor—the penthouse.

Reva usually preferred to drive. She liked the control, the solitude, and the ability to blast music or sit in silence, depending on her mood. But today had been a long day, packed with back-to-back meetings and calls that couldn't wait. Rather than deal with the hassle of navigating traffic while juggling work, she had opted for convenience.

Her father's chauffeur, Ramesh, was a familiar presence—efficient, unobtrusive, and well-versed in Gurugram's traffic snarls. It helped that he knew when to keep quiet and when to offer a comment about the city's ever-growing chaos.

Besides, parking in the city was a nightmare, especially during office hours. Even in her own apartment complex, it could take longer than she liked. This way, as Ramesh dealt with the logistics, she could just step out at the entrance, while having some time to catch up on last-minute emails before heading to—

Her thoughts stuttered as the car neared her apartment complex.

She stilled, her gaze flicking outside the car window. Across the garden, past the swimming pool of the complex, he lived in the building right across from hers.

The realization sent a strange ripple through her.

Her first instinct was still to refuse. She wasn't in the mood for another battle tonight. But curiosity tugged at her.

How did he live? Was it as sleek and controlled as his office? Or was there something more personal lurking beneath that polished exterior?

And, though she wouldn't admit it, another question burned at the back of her mind.

Who did he live with?

Who was the person he got pastries for?

She shook her head. *Not your business, Reva.*

But still, she hesitated before responding.

Reva Khanna: *Fine. But just so you know, this is beyond conventional work timings. Some of us have a life.*

His reply came almost instantly.

Angad Sareen: *But you were the one who asked for flexible timings. If I remember correctly, it was one of your conditions.*

Reva scowled at the screen, fingers poised to fire back a response.

Meanwhile, Angad leaned back in his chair, phone in hand, the ghost of a smile tugging at his lips. Flexible timing—her demand, not his. And yet, here she was, calling him out for it.

Still, he found himself wondering—how exactly did she spend her time beyond work?

More importantly, *with whom?*

Reva Khanna: *No, you make others work beyond conventional office timings. That's different.*

A beat. Then—

Angad Sareen: *Do I? Or do I just know how to pick people for whom 'work matters.' People like you.*

Reva's fingers tightened around her phone. He threw her words back at her. Oh, he was good.

Reva Khanna: *Flattery won't get me there faster.*

Angad Sareen: *It wasn't flattery. Just an observation.*

Reva rolled her eyes, already regretting engaging in this conversation.

Before she could type a reply, another message popped up.

Angad Sareen: *And before you argue further, this can't wait until tomorrow. There's a critical issue with the website that needs immediate attention.*

Her fingers hovered over the keyboard, debating whether to push back.

Angad Sareen: *Also, I can't leave home for personal reasons, so we're doing this here.*

Reva frowned, curiosity prickling at her. *Personal reasons?* He didn't seem like the type to mix work and home life. What was so important that he had to work from home?

Not that it mattered. What mattered was that this man—this insufferable man—had a way of making her bend to his will.

With a resigned sigh, she tapped out her response.

Reva Khanna: *Fine. See you at 6:30.*

She locked her phone, but the questions still lingered. What personal reason? And more importantly... who was at home waiting for him?

Reva exhaled through her nose, fighting the ridiculous flutter in her stomach.

She shouldn't be going. She should set boundaries and make it clear that after a certain hour, she wasn't at his beck and call.

Reva sighed, running a hand through her hair as she glanced at her watch. 6:15 PM.

Gurugram's rush hour had taken its toll, eating away at her time. She didn't have time to go home to change into something more comfortable. She might as well get this over with—finish the meeting at Angad's and then finally retreat into the quiet of her own space.

She leaned forward when Ramesh stopped the car in front of their building, catching his attention. "Drop me off at Building Number 9 instead. Across from ours."

The older man's brows furrowed in the rearview mirror. "Not going home, Didi?"

She shook her head, already typing a quick message. "No, I have an urgent meeting. Let Maa and Papa know I won't join them and Sanaya for dinner tonight."

Ramesh nodded. "Should I wait for you there?"

She hesitated for a moment, then exhaled. "No. I'll walk back."

The last thing she wanted was to drag this night out any longer than necessary. She just wanted to get this meeting done, step into the quiet of her own apartment, and finally—*finally*—end this day.

***

CHAPTER EIGHT

THE REALIZATION

Reva arrived a few minutes earlier, her nerves buzzing with an unease she didn't quite understand. She wasn't intimidated by Angad Sareen—not in the traditional sense. But something about being alone with him in his personal space unsettled her. Their work dynamic was already complicated enough; she didn't need the added layer of his home, his presence, his world bleeding into hers.

But the moment the elevator doors slid open to his penthouse floor, she realized she wouldn't be alone with him after all.

'An all business' Angad, she noted.

He was dressed in blue denims and a plain white shirt—effortless yet infuriatingly good-looking. If she had thought he looked sharp in a business suit, it had nothing on this. She didn't think she could have a fetish for a guy in jeans, but apparently, Angad Sareen was testing that theory.

"Reva." He stepped forward, gesturing for her to come in. "Thanks for coming. And apologies for the last-minute call, and the location."

She moved inside, her gaze flicking around the space. She immediately noticed how different it felt from a corporate office. The penthouse was striking yet understated, exuding a quiet elegance that felt entirely in line with the man who owned it.

His dining table had been converted into a temporary boardroom, strewn with laptops, printed layouts, and half-full coffee cups. Amit and Neha, two key members of the design and content team, were already there, deep in discussion over a set of mockups.

Angad returned to stand at the head of the table, sleeves rolled up, a tablet in hand. He looked every bit the composed businessman, except for the slight tension in his posture—something only noticeable if one was paying close attention. And Reva was.

His was the last corner building in the complex—private, perfectly positioned. Inside, marble floors gleamed under the soft glow of ambient lighting, and the furniture was elegant. The far side opened up to sweeping views of the golf course, its manicured greens glowing under floodlights as evening games unfolded. On the other end, a wide balcony stretched out into the hush of twilight. Reva knew that if she stepped onto it, she'd spot her own building just across the central garden—where the clubhouse stood nestled among play structures and the still water of the swimming pool. Beyond that, the gentle hum of Golf Course Road threaded faintly through the silence, a distant reminder of the city's heartbeat. Despite its polished surfaces and curated charm, the space felt unexpectedly warm. Real. Like someone had started laying the foundations of a life here—quietly, thoughtfully.

"I couldn't leave the house today," he continued, his voice matter-of-fact. "I've been working from here since morning. It was urgent, so I had to call you here."

There was something in the way he said it—without elaboration, without excuse—that made her pause. A quiet curiosity stirred in her, but she didn't ask. Instead, she nodded, setting her bag down at the table.

Angad's gaze ran over her, taking in the way she was still in work attire. "Straight from work?" he asked.

She nodded. "Had a meeting before this. I was just on my way home when you buzzed."

His brows lifted slightly. "And have you had anything to eat?"

That caught her off guard. He was staring at her with a mix of curiosity and something that almost resembled concern.

"I—" She paused, realizing she hadn't. The day had been a blur of meetings and deadlines.

Angad exhaled, shaking his head. "I'll have something brought in."

"It's fine," she started to protest, but he was already turning to someone in the kitchen, issuing instructions.

Reva folded her arms, watching him. There was something unsettling about seeing him like this—less the ruthless businessman, more… human.

"Let's get started, then," she said, pulling her focus back to work.

*

The meeting was as intense as Reva had expected. Amit and Neha presented the latest design and content drafts, while Angad methodically went through every detail, his focus razor-sharp. His ability to pick apart inconsistencies, challenge weak arguments, and demand better was both impressive and infuriating. He wasn't cruel—just relentless.

Reva matched his energy, pushing back when necessary. The editorial direction had to be engaging, she argued. The audience wasn't looking for just facts; they wanted analysis, depth, and nuance. Angad countered, pointing out that too much embellishment would dilute the credibility of the news portal.

It was a dance, back and forth. One they had engaged in before, but something about tonight made it feel more charged. Maybe it was the setting, maybe it was the casualness of his attire, or maybe it was simply the fact that she was becoming more attuned to him in ways she wasn't sure she wanted to be.

At some point, one of the staff members discreetly placed a plate of sandwiches and coffee beside her. Angad didn't say anything, didn't so much as glance her way. But somehow, that small, practical gesture—quietly thoughtful—unsettled her more than all the arguments they'd had.

As the meeting progressed, Reva couldn't help but notice that Angad kept coming and going through one of the doors. It was subtle, almost instinctive, but there was a pull—something behind that door that needed his attention. She wondered what or who it led to.

By the time they wrapped up, the tension had given way to a grudging satisfaction. Even Angad, for all his stubbornness, seemed pleased with the progress. Amit gathered his laptop, stretching.

"That was productive," he admitted. "I'll make the changes to the design flow and send them across by morning."

Neha yawned. "Same here. I'll refine the headlines and send the updated draft."

Angad gave them both a nod. "Good work. Get some rest."

As Amit and Neha packed up their things, murmuring their goodbyes, Reva leaned back in her chair, rolling the tension from her shoulders. The meeting had been productive—surprisingly so—but she was more than ready to leave. She had spent the entire evening navigating ideas, debates, and the undercurrent of whatever strange energy always existed between her and Angad.

She reached for her bag, but before she could stand, his voice cut through the air, low and firm.

"Reva, stay back for a minute. I want to discuss something further."

She looked up, brows slightly raised. Amit and Neha glanced at each other before exchanging a look and excusing themselves, letting the door click shut behind them.

Silence settled over the room.

Angad exhaled, gripping the edge of the dining table. He didn't know why he had stopped her, what he wanted to say. Just that he wasn't ready for her to go.

She was here. In his home. His personal space.

And yet, he didn't feel uncomfortable.

He looked at her, really looked at her—starting from the heels she still had on, up the curve of her legs, the slight crease in her blouse from sitting too long, the way a loose strand of hair had fallen over her cheek.

Then he met her eyes.

Questioning.

Waiting.

Oh. He had to say something.

Had to give her a reason why he'd asked her to stay.

Reva cut through the awkward silence. "Is everything okay?"

Angad's jaw ticked, his posture still tense, as if he was debating something internally.

"Do you often work from home?" she asked, hoping to steer the conversation toward safer ground.

Before he could respond, a small voice interrupted them—high-pitched and distressed.

"Daddy!"

Reva turned just in time to see a little girl running toward Angad, her dark curls bouncing with each hurried step. Tears streaked her round cheeks, her lower lip trembling.

"Anika," Angad murmured, his entire demeanor shifting in an instant. The controlled businessman disappeared, replaced by something softer, something infinitely more human.

But Anika didn't stop at her father. Instead, she ran straight to Reva.

"Reedi!" she squealed, wrapping her tiny arms around Reva's legs.

Reva froze, utterly blindsided.

Her eyes darted to the man standing across the room. He was a dad.

Angad's expression transformed—from confusion to shock to something unreadable. She's the woman his kids can't stop raving about.

"You're... *Riddhi*?" he asked, his voice gruff.

Reva frowned. "Who is Riddhi?"

Angad's jaw clenched. "That's what they call you, don't they? Why did you lie to them about your name?"

She blinked, trying to process—and then realization dawned. The twins had overheard Trisha calling her *Ree Di* and mistook it for her name. And Angad, in his assumption-laced protectiveness, thought she had lied to them.

She exhaled, shaking her head. "No, they heard my cousin calling me *Ree Di* – short for *Reva Didi*. And started calling me that."

Angad's gaze didn't soften. If anything, the unreadable emotion in his eyes deepened—something guarded. Protective. Questioning.

They both had questions. Oh, so many of them.

Before they could process it further, Anika tugged at Reva's hand, her tiny fingers curling around hers as she looked between her and Angad, her big, hopeful eyes full of innocent curiosity.

"So, you know her, Daddy?" Anika asked, tilting her head. "She's not a stranger anymore? And I can go to her house and play with her?"

Angad was speechless for a second, blindsided by the child's logic. He inhaled sharply and came closer to where Anika and Reva were standing. He bent down to Anika's level, his hands resting lightly on her small shoulders.

"First, tell me, baby, how are you feeling now?" His voice softened in a way that Reva had never heard before. "Did you sleep well? It looks like the fever is gone. But do you still have the stomach ouchie?" He pressed a hand lightly to her forehead, smiling at her.

Reva watched them, something tugging at her heart in a way she hadn't expected.

This wasn't the Angad Sareen she had come to know—the sharp-witted businessman, the ruthless negotiator, the man who never backed down from a challenge.

This was Angad Sareen—the dad.

And then it hit her suddenly. Avik's words echoed in her mind: *We don't have a mother.*

He wasn't just their dad.

He was their *single* dad.

Her breath hitched for a moment as the truth settled in, heavier than she expected. The pastries had been for his kids. The softened tone in his voice—meant for them. And yet, despite everything, a wave of relief washed over her. Why did that matter so much? Why did it ease something she hadn't even realized was tense?

"No, Daddy. I'm better now. Can I play with Reedi? Is she still a stranger?" Anika's voice cut through her spiraling thoughts, pulling her back to the moment.

Angad glanced at her, then shifted his eyes back to Anika, his expression once again giving nothing away.

"No, darling," he said, his voice gentle but firm. "She's not a stranger." His eyes flicked back to Reva, watching her closely. "And yes, you can go to her house to play… *if she's okay with it.*"

His words hung in the air, deliberate, weighted with something unspoken.

Reva met his gaze briefly before crouching down to Anika's level, her hands resting on her knees. She smiled at the little girl, brushing a stray curl away from her face.

"Of course, sweetheart," she said softly. "You're always welcome at my place. Both you and Avik." She glanced at Angad, then back at Anika. "Sanaya would be very happy to have you over."

Angad watched the exchange, something shifting inside him.

Something dangerous.

Something he couldn't afford to feel.

He had spent years compartmentalizing, keeping his personal life locked away from everything else. But watching Reva interact with Anika—so naturally, so gently—something inside him cracked.

She looked like she belonged here.

And that thought terrified him.

He forced himself to refocus, to push away whatever the hell was happening inside him.

"So, you live in this complex?" he asked, his voice coming out more gruffly than he intended.

Reva nodded. "Yes."

His brows furrowed. "Then… what were you doing at their school?"

She shifted, clearly uneasy—a rare crack in her usually composed demeanor.

Reva wasn't the kind of person who flaunted her background. She carried her privilege with quiet dignity, never using it as a crutch or an advantage.

"I'm a board member," she said quietly. "The school is owned by my family. It's named after my grandfather—Sham Lal Khanna."

Angad stilled.

The name struck him with unexpected weight. Sham Lal Khanna wasn't just any name—it carried a legacy, influence, and wealth of a caliber few could match. He had assumed she was well-off, successful in her own right, but this… this was something else.

"And Meera Ahuja, the principal?" he asked after a beat. "Do you know her?"

Reva's lips pressed together before she nodded. "Yes," she admitted. "She's my aunt."

His expression shifted the sharp scrutiny in his eyes, giving way to something quieter. Something closer to respect.

She had never once flaunted it. Never wielded her family name as a weapon or a privilege. She had worked alongside them, held her ground, earned her place—not because of where she came from, but because of who she had made herself.

Watching her kneel beside his daughter, pausing before she spoke, something shifted within him.

She was no longer just the woman who intrigued him—she was someone he respected.

A stretch of silence followed—awkward, heavy, filled with unspoken thoughts neither of them knew how to voice.

Before either could break it, Raju appeared in the doorway, clearing his throat hesitantly.

"Sir," he said, addressing Angad. "Lata Didi called. Avik Baba is refusing to come out of the pool, and she doesn't want to leave him alone."

Angad exhaled, running a hand down his face, looking visibly torn.

His gaze shifted between Anika, now holding Reva's hand tightly, and the main door.

He was being pulled in two directions again—an ache he knew too well.

He hated it.

But he couldn't be in two places at once.

His eyes settled on Reva again.

"Could you please stay with her for just a little while?" His voice was quieter now, lower in tone. "Let me go get Avik."

It wasn't just a request.

It was trust.

And for reasons she couldn't quite explain, Reva nodded.

***

CHAPTER NINE

FAMILY DINNER TIME

Angad strode into the clubhouse pool area, the scent of chlorine thick in the warm evening air. Lata stood off to the side, wringing her hands, her expression caught between exasperation and helplessness. Avik floated on his back in the water, utterly unbothered, kicking lazily to stay afloat.

The moment Angad stepped closer, his son's eyes flicked to him, wary and knowing.

"Avik," Angad called, his tone even but firm. "It's time to come out."

Avik narrowed his eyes, shook his head, and kept floating.

Angad sighed. He had expected this. His son was just as stubborn as he was. "You've been in there long enough."

"Five more minutes," Avik countered immediately.

"Now."

Avik pouted, still making no move to obey. Lata cast Angad an uncertain glance, but he merely crouched by the pool's edge, lowering his voice. "There's a surprise waiting for you at home."

That got his attention. Avik stilled, eyes darting toward him in suspicion. "What kind of surprise?"

"If I tell you, it won't be a surprise anymore, will it?" Angad smirked slightly.

Avik huffed, clearly debating whether or not to trust him. Finally, with exaggerated reluctance, he swam to the edge of the pool. "Fine."

Angad took the towel from Lata and wrapped it around his son as he climbed out. "Dry up. We're leaving in two minutes."

Avik grumbled under his breath, but complied, rubbing his hair roughly as he trudged toward the locker room to change.

Angad exhaled, standing straight again. He had won this round, but the boy was getting smarter, harder to negotiate with.

And then, without warning, an image flashed in his mind—Reva, kneeling beside Anika, her voice gentle yet firm, her eyes warm yet hesitant.

Reva. In his house. With his daughter.

A place she didn't belong. And yet… it hadn't felt wrong.

It felt okay.

No, more than okay. It felt good.

And that realization—that dangerous, impossible realization—settled deep in his chest, filling him with warmth. And, simultaneously, terrifying him to his core.

He had spent years crafting boundaries, ensuring his personal life stayed untouched—sealed off from anyone outside his world. His children were his only priority. His focus, unshakable.

But something shifted the moment Reva Khanna stepped into his home.

She had looked like she belonged there. And that was going to be a problem.

Shaking off the thought, Angad glanced toward the locker rooms, waiting for Avik to emerge. Lata approached hesitantly, her voice low with concern.

"Sir, Anika Baby is still sleeping? Is your meeting over? Is she alone?"

Angad exhaled, his lips tilting in something between amusement and disbelief. "No, Lata. Their 'Riddhi' has been found. She's with Anika."

Lata's brows knitted together in confusion, her mouth opening as if to ask something, but she thought better of it. She merely nodded, though the curiosity in her eyes lingered.

Before Angad could dwell on it further, Avik came bouncing out of the locker room, dressed in dry clothes, his hair still damp.

"Ready?" Angad asked, shaking off his thoughts.

Avik shrugged. "I guess. If the surprise is good."

Angad chuckled, ruffling his son's hair despite his protests. "Let's go."

As they stepped out into the cool night, his mind circled back to the woman waiting at home.

His initial plan had been simple—finish the meeting, dinner, stories, bedtime. But now, with Reva still there, with the twins clearly attached to her…

For once, he didn't quite know what to expect.

*

Reva sat cross-legged on the plush rug in the living room, her fingers idly brushing over the fabric of Anika's favorite stuffed bunny as the little girl chattered on about her toys. The soft hum of the air conditioner filled the room, blending with Anika's delighted giggles as she introduced each stuffed animal with an enthusiasm that made Reva smile.

But even as she listened, her mind kept drifting.

To him.

Angad Sareen—the man, and then Angad Sareen—the father.

She had only known him in professional settings—stern, unyielding, calculating. A man who commanded rooms, not just with his presence but with the sharp precision of his words. But here, in this space that belonged entirely to him, she was beginning to see something else. Something more.

She had seen it in the way he had spoken to Anika, the way he had crouched to her level, and softened his voice. The way he had listened to her with quiet patience, making her feel heard, important. There was something unshakably steady in him, something deeply protective.

There was patience in him. A deep, unwavering protectiveness.

And yet, something was still missing.

Reva's fingers stilled on the soft fur of the bunny. *Where was their mother?*

Avik's words from earlier echoed again in her mind: '*We don't have a mother.*'

The words had been spoken so simply, without the weight of longing or sadness. Just a fact. Plain and unwavering.

It made her very, very curious. She noticed photos of the three of them in the living room, but not a single sign of the mother. Not even one picture.

Before she could dwell on it further, a small hand tugged at hers. "Reedi, I want to show you my room!" Anika declared, eyes wide with excitement.

Reva laughed softly. "Alright, lead the way."

Anika eagerly dragged her down the hallway, pausing before a door painted in soft pastel pink. She pushed it open dramatically, revealing a space straight out of a fairytale.

The room was a blend of dreamy pinks and whites, with a canopy bed draped in sheer lace standing at its center. Stuffed animals of all shapes and sizes lined the shelves, an entire corner dedicated to dolls. Twinkling star-shaped lights were strung along the walls, casting a warm glow over the space. A large framed picture of Anika and Avik hung above the bed, their grinning faces captured mid-laughter.

"This is beautiful, Anika," Reva said genuinely, stepping inside. The room was a reflection of the little girl who had so easily taken up space in her heart—bright, warm, full of wonder.

Anika beamed. "Do you like it? Look, I even have a tea set! We can have a tea party."

"I'd love that," Reva said, sitting down beside the tiny play table. But before she could pick up the delicate pink teacup, Anika was already tugging at her hand again.

"Come see Avik's room!"

Reva let herself be pulled along, following the little girl down the hall to the next door. This one was a stark contrast to the first.

Avik's room was blue and gray, a space designed for adventure rather than fairytales. A large bunk bed took center stage, with neatly arranged superhero posters covering the walls. A collection of toy cars and action figures was lined up meticulously on a shelf, and the floor was scattered with books—some open, others stacked in uneven piles.

"He likes cars," Anika said conspiratorially. "He says he's too old for stuffed toys now."

Reva chuckled. "I think he's at that age where he wants to be cool."

Anika giggled. "But he still hugs his dinosaur teddy when he sleeps. Don't tell him I told you!"

Reva laughed, raising a hand as if to swear secrecy. "I won't."

But just as she was about to suggest they head back, Anika grabbed her hand once more.

"Now, Daddy's room!"

Reva blinked, suddenly hesitating. "Anika... maybe we should wait for your daddy."

But Anika was already dragging her forward. "It's okay! Come!"

She had no choice but to follow as the little girl pushed open the heavy wooden door.

The moment Reva stepped inside, something shifted in her.

Angad's room was exactly as she had expected it to be—minimalistic, neat, controlled. The color scheme was a deep mix of charcoal, navy, and white, the furniture sleek and modern. A large bed with crisp sheets took center stage, and a bookshelf lined one wall, filled with biographies, finance books, and legal journals. There were no personal photographs, no unnecessary decor, only the bare essentials.

Yet, despite its lack of warmth, it felt like him.

Commanding. Private. Untouchable.

She felt like an intruder just standing there.

Anika, oblivious to her hesitation, ran toward the bed and flopped onto it, making herself comfortable. "This is where Daddy sleeps!" she announced proudly.

Reva swallowed. An image flashed through her mind—Angad sleeping on that very bed, his ruffled hair a stark contrast to his usual polished appearance. He wore no shirt, and the covers pooled just below his navel. She dared not let her imagination take her further.

Her eyes drifted to the large desk near the window. Papers were stacked in organized piles, a laptop sat open, and a crystal glass with a trace of amber liquid rested beside it.

She wasn't sure why, but standing here felt intimate. More intimate than it should have been.

Her heart thudded.

This wasn't just any room.

This was his room.

And she had no business being in it.

But before she could step back, before she could remind herself that this was not her place, Anika looked up at her with innocent eyes and said, "Daddy will be so happy you're here."

Reva's breath caught.

Will he?

She wasn't so sure.

Her mind had wandered—dangerously so. The image of Angad lying on this very bed, sheets rumpled around his waist, his hair mussed from sleep, had taken root in her thoughts. She had no business picturing him like that. No business imagining what it would feel like to lie next to him, to feel his warmth, the rough scrape of his stubble against her skin—

A sharp intake of breath made her whirl around.

Angad stood in the doorway.

Her heart lurched.

He was there. Watching her. His expression was calm, but his eyes—oh, his eyes. Dark. Intense. Burning.

And then, he swallowed.

She saw the way his throat bobbed, the way his fingers curled into fists at his sides. He was standing still, yet she could feel the tension rolling off him in waves. And she knew. Knew exactly where his mind had gone.

Because she had been there too.

The image of her in his bed, tangled in his sheets, in *him*—it flickered across his face like a forbidden thought he had no right entertaining.

And yet, it was there. Between them. Electric. Dangerous.

A delighted squeak shattered the moment.

"Reedi!" Avik's voice rang out, breaking the silence like a crack of lightning. The little boy darted forward with an enthusiasm that caught her off guard, his arms flinging around her waist in sheer excitement.

Reva barely had a second to brace herself before the force of his hug sent her stumbling back.

Onto the bed.

She landed with a soft bounce, her back hitting the mattress, her body sinking into the space she had been so vividly imagining only moments ago. Anika shrieked with laughter, and Avik giggled against her stomach, clearly delighted by his own mischief.

But Reva?

Reva was mortified.

Her entire face flamed as she scrambled upright, her hands pressing into the sheets as if they burned. Her eyes darted up—only to meet Angad's.

Oh God.

His jaw was locked, his shoulders tense, his chest rising and falling just a little too quickly. And lower—

No, don't look lower.

But it was too late. She had already noticed the way his stance had shifted, the subtle clench of his fingers, the way his breath had hitched just a fraction.

A flash of something dark and primal stirred in his gaze.

And then, just as quickly as it appeared, it was gone.

Angad cleared his throat, his voice rougher than usual. "It's dinner time, kids."

Reva scrambled to her feet, brushing imaginary wrinkles from her outfit, her cheeks still burning. "I—I didn't mean to come in here," she stammered. "Anika just—"

"I know," he cut her off, his voice gruff. He ran a hand over his jaw, looking anywhere but at her. "It's fine."

Except it wasn't fine. The air between them was thick, charged, humming with something neither of them was ready to name.

Anika tugged at his hand. "Daddy, can Reedi stay for dinner?"

Avik perked up instantly. "Yes! Please, Daddy! Please!"

Angad hesitated. His eyes met Reva's, searching. A moment passed. Then another.

"Ask her."

The kids clasped her hands, pleading. "Please, Reedi! Stay!"

Reva hesitated.

Angad held her gaze. "Look, it's dinner time," he repeated, his voice quiet but firm. "The kids would be very happy if you stayed."

Reva wasn't sure it was a good idea—not after what had just passed between them. But before she could find an excuse, Angad arched a brow and said, "Please stay… unless someone is waiting for you back home."

Reva hesitated for a fraction of a second before shaking her head lightly. "No, there's no one waiting for me." Then she turned to the kids, laughing, "Alright, alright, I'll stay."

Angad exhaled a breath he didn't know he was holding.

Excited, the kids grabbed her hands and led her out. But as they approached the dining table, the remnants of the meeting were still scattered there, making it look more like a boardroom than a place for a family meal.

Angad frowned. "Raju," he called. "Lay the table in the living room tonight."

Raju blinked in surprise but nodded. "Yes, sir."

Soon, dinner was served in the cozy room. Anika and Avik both plopped onto the sofa, one on each side of Reva. Angad took the seat on the side of the sofa, his gaze lingering on the three of them.

His chest tightened with a yearning he hadn't felt in years.

For a moment, he let himself imagine it. What if this wasn't temporary? What if, just this once, he let himself believe it could be more?

But that was a dangerous thought.

One he wasn't ready for.

*

Avik and Anika kept up a steady stream of chatter throughout dinner, their voices animated as they shared stories with Reva.

"Raju bhaiya doesn't know how to make good mac and cheese," Anika declared with a pout, pushing a spoon through her rice. "We used to have the best one in New York."

Avik nodded in agreement. "Yeah. It was creamy, and cheesy, and sooo good. The ones here are… just okay."

Reva smiled. "Maybe I can teach Raju bhaiya a trick or two."

"Do you know how to cook mac and cheese?" Anika beamed.

"Yes, I do," Reva replied with a grin. "I'll make some for you guys soon."

Anika clapped her hands excitedly while Avik shifted gears. "I miss our old nanny," he murmured, his voice quieter. "She used to make the best mac and cheese and tell us the best stories. She even cried when she dropped us at the airport."

Angad's hand stilled on his fork, his jaw tightening slightly at the mention of New York. He remained impassive, but Reva didn't miss the tension in his posture—or the wary glint that passed through his eyes. Reva's heart squeezed at that. She offered Avik a small, reassuring smile. "She must have loved you both a lot."

"She did," Avik confirmed before diving into another story about their time in New York.

Reva kept up the conversation, nodding and smiling in all the right places, though her eyes kept straying to Angad. He was unusually quiet, his focus on his plate, eating with deliberate, unhurried movements. It was a stark contrast to the vibrant energy of his children.

The evening passed in warm conversation and playful laughter, but eventually, Lata entered, her presence a silent reminder that it was time for bed.

"*Chalo*, Anika baby, Avik baba," she said gently. "Time to sleep."

Anika's face fell. "But I don't want to sleep."

Avik folded his arms. "Me neither."

Reva chuckled. "You have school tomorrow, don't you?"

The twins exchanged a look before sighing in resignation. But before they left, they turned to Reva with pleading eyes.

"Promise you'll come back tomorrow?" Anika asked, her voice hopeful.

Avik nodded. "You have to come, Reedi."

Reva hesitated, feeling Angad's gaze on her, but then she smiled. "Okay, I promise."

Satisfied, the kids hugged her before Lata ushered them away. As their footsteps faded, Reva got up to leave.

"Thank you for dinner. I should head home," she said.

Angad stood as well. "I'll drop you."

Reva shook her head. "I live five minutes away—just across the park, in building three. I'll walk down. This is the safest society in Gurugram." Then, with a teasing glint in her eyes, she added, "No 'stranger' can come in to kidnap me."

Angad let out a soft laugh, rubbing the back of his neck. "Yeah… about that. I may have overreacted."

Reva waved off his apology. "I get why you did it."

They stepped outside together, the evening air crisp and quiet around them as they strolled toward her building. The easy silence between them felt… comfortable.

After a beat, Reva smirked. "You know, it looks like you're always feeding me. I should return the favor soon."

Angad shot her a sideways glance, a slow, intrigued smile forming. "Careful, Reva. That sounds dangerously close to a dinner invitation."

She arched a brow. "And if it is?"

His smirk deepened, but he didn't answer right away. Instead, he let the anticipation linger before saying, "Then I'd have to accept."

They reached her building, and the conversation faded into an awkward yet oddly pleasant silence. Their gazes held for a beat too long, something unsaid stretching between them.

Finally, Angad cleared his throat. "Thank you for staying back with Anika tonight."

Reva nodded, offering a small smile. "Goodnight, Angad."

He watched as she stepped inside, resisting the inexplicable urge to call her back.

Instead, he turned around and walked away, that lingering warmth still curling inside his chest.

***

CHAPTER TEN

THE PAST

Reva curled up on her plush sofa, a warm cup of chamomile tea cradled between her hands, but her mind was far from the soothing warmth it provided after a long, *no,* a very long day. Instead, it was occupied with thoughts of Angad Sareen.

Not the powerful businessman. Not the arrogant, imposing man she had first met. But Angad—the father.

She had seen many men in her life—powerful, wealthy, and entitled. Men who wielded their last names and fortunes like weapons, just as Manish had. But Angad?

Reva had never thought of Angad Sareen as a father.

A businessman. A man who commanded attention the moment he walked into a room. A man who had the kind of arrogance that came naturally to those who had built empires with their bare hands. Yes, she had imagined all those things about him. But a father? A present, engaged, and deeply devoted father? That had never crossed her mind.

Yet, tonight, she had seen it. Felt it.

And it rattled her.

The way his children clung to him, the way their eyes lit up when he spoke, the way he—this powerful, seemingly untouchable man—softened for them, indulged their endless chatter, listened like their words were the most important thing in the world. He wasn't just responsible for them; he was theirs in a way that had nothing to do with duty and everything to do with love.

She had watched him move through the evening with an ease that made her chest tighten. How effortlessly he had handled their moods, their questions, their playful defiance. There was no impatience, no distraction, no moment where he seemed eager to be anywhere else. He was there. Fully. Completely.

And then, the realization hit her—he had shifted his entire workday home today because Anika wasn't well. Because his daughter had needed him, he had put everything else aside without hesitation. Just like that.

A lump formed in her throat at the thought.

Because it reminded her of her own loving dad, who used to be like that when she was a child. Hell, he's like that even now! And suddenly, she saw it—how Angad, the father, was so much like her own. The best of men.

The warmth, the laughter, the way Anika and Avik had nestled against her like she belonged there... It had been dangerously easy to fall into it, to forget, just for a moment, that this wasn't her place. That she wasn't part of this little world he had built.

But for a heartbeat, it had felt like she was.

And that was the most dangerous feeling of all.

Because Reva knew better than to long for things that weren't meant to be hers.

And Angad Sareen, with his children, his quiet devotion, and eyes that revealed nothing—he wasn't meant to be hers either.

But something had shifted. Suddenly, she wasn't so sure she wanted to remember that.

She exhaled slowly, pushing the thoughts away, but one lingered at the edge of her mind—Anika.

She made a mental note to check on her in the morning.

But even as she tried to settle her mind, Avik's small voice echoed back at her—*We don't have a mother.*

No mother. Just Angad. Raising two children alone. How? Why?

Reva sighed, leaning back into the couch. It wasn't just Angad's past that haunted her thoughts. Her own ghosts lurked in the corners of her mind, refusing to be ignored.

Manish.

The name alone sent a bitter taste to her tongue.

She had once believed in forever. She had once believed in love. She had once believed that she was enough.

Until she wasn't.

Manish had come from *new money*—the kind that dripped with the desperate need to prove itself. The kind that measured success not by character but by the number of zeros in a bank account and the luxury labels stitched on clothes and accessories. For him, wealth wasn't just a privilege; it was power. And power, in his world, meant that rules—commitment, fidelity, loyalty—were optional.

Reva had been too blind, too naïve to see it back then.

She had thought they were in love. Thought he had chosen *her.* But she had been nothing more than a stepping stone, a golden pass into the circles he wanted to be a part of. She was *Reva Khanna*—daughter of an old-money business family, with connections that could open doors he would have never reached on his own.

And in the end, he hadn't even bothered to hide the truth.

She had caught them *together*, tangled in each other, lips locked, bodies pressed, *on her own birthday.*

Five years ago.

It was supposed to have been *their* night. The one night that was about her, about them. She had been excited, nervous even, hoping maybe—*just maybe*—he had planned something special. Instead, she had walked in on him with *her*—the younger, thinner, effortlessly beautiful woman who had never needed to try.

That moment had rewritten everything.

When she had confronted him, the man she had loved, the man she had thought would be her future, he hadn't even had the decency to be ashamed.

"Reva, don't be dramatic. You and I both know this was never about love."

The words had shattered something inside her, but it was his next admission that had crushed whatever was left.

"Let's be honest—if you weren't Reva ***Khanna****, do you really think I would have even looked at you twice?"*

Her stomach had dropped.

She had known, deep down, that their relationship had its cracks, that he had been changing, pulling away. But she had *never* expected this level of cruelty.

That night, Manish hadn't just broken her trust. He had shattered her self-worth.

She had been *convenient.* An easy way up the ladder. And once he had climbed high enough, he had no use for her anymore.

The woman he had chosen over her had been everything she wasn't—*slender, effortlessly gorgeous, desirable in ways Reva had never felt she could be.*

And suddenly, she had seen it all so clearly—he had never looked at *her* that way. Never with hunger, never with awe. Never like he wanted her beyond what she could offer him.

She had *never* been enough.

That night had changed her. Not just in how she viewed love, but in how she viewed *herself.*

Even now, five years later, after rebuilding her life, after proving herself in a world where she was more than just a last name—those insecurities lingered. She had spent years ensuring that her family name wasn't the first thing people associated with her, that her worth wasn't tied to the wealth she had been born into. Because she knew now—*knew painfully well*—that people who cared about her background more than her *as a person* would never truly see *her.*

Manish had taken so much from her.

But she had taken something back.

Herself.

And yet, there were still moments, still nights like these, where the past reared its ugly head, whispering cruel reminders of all the ways she had once been *not enough.*

So why was Angad Sareen—the formidable, arrogant, commanding man—making her feel seen? Making her feel something she had long buried?

Reva took a deep breath, shaking her head. No. She wasn't going down this path again.

But, as her eyes drifted to the soft glow of the floodlights in the golf course outside her window, she knew one thing for sure—Angad Sareen was beginning to feel dangerously close to something she had sworn she'd never let herself feel again.

*

Angad leaned against the bar in his penthouse, a glass of whiskey swirling in his hand. The silence of his home was almost deafening, save for the faint sounds of the city beyond his windows.

Reva had been in his home.

With his kids.

In his bedroom.

His jaw clenched as the image flooded his mind—her standing there, caught in his space, her face flushed, her eyes wide with embarrassment.

And the way she had fallen onto his bed, laughing with his children, completely at ease in a place no other woman had ever been.

Something inside him twisted at the thought.

It felt good.

And that terrified him to the core.

His fingers tightened around the glass as he exhaled sharply. He needed to stop this train of thought. Needed to push her out of his mind.

But the way she had been with Avik and Anika...

Natural.

Effortless.

Like she belonged.

A sharp pang hit his chest, one he wasn't ready to acknowledge. His kids deserved a mother. A nurturing, present mother. But they had never had one. They had only had him.

And that was his doing.

His thoughts drifted back to the past, back to the moment that had changed everything.

Bridgette.

American. Brunette. Hazel-green eyes—the same green that reflected back at him every time he looked at his children.

One night. That was all it had been. One reckless night, fueled by alcohol and the arrogance of youth. He had been untouchable back then. Power consumed him, and success ran through his veins. He had been invincible.

Until she had come back weeks later, telling him she was pregnant.

His first reaction had been disbelief. Then anger. Then panic. He wasn't ready. He had never planned for this.

But none of that had mattered. Because Bridgette had been clear—she didn't want the baby. She wanted money. She was going to terminate the pregnancy. She had a career, dreams, ambitions. A child had no place in that.

That was the moment Angad decided.

He told her to give him one year. One year to carry the child. Then she could walk away, no strings attached. He would take care of everything.

She had hesitated, but when he had put an ironclad contract in front of her—one that came with a hefty financial incentive—she agreed.

Neither of them had expected twins.

When they found out, Bridgette demanded more money, and he gave it without a second thought. She delivered, signed the final papers, took the money, and disappeared without ever looking back.

Angad had been left with two tiny, helpless lives in his arms and a terrifying realization—*he had no idea how to be a father.*

He had never planned for it. Never imagined himself in this role.

One moment, he was living the life he had meticulously built—power, wealth, influence—all at his fingertips. Next, he was staring down at two newborns, their tiny fingers curling instinctively around his, their soft cries filling the sterile hospital room.

He had been overwhelmed. Terrified, even.

What did he know about parenting? About late-night feedings, colic, and lullabies? He had built companies from the ground up, managed teams, and made high-stakes decisions that had shaped industries—*but this? This* was something else entirely.

He had stood there, watching Bridgette sign away her parental rights with an ease that made his stomach turn. She had barely looked at them—at *him*. Just took the check, her body already half-turned toward the door, toward the life she had been so desperate to return to.

"They're all yours," she had said, almost flippantly, before walking away.

And just like that, she was gone.

Leaving *him* behind.

Alone.

With *them.*

Two perfect, fragile souls who had no one in the world but *him.*

For the second time in his life, Angad had felt utterly lost. The first time was when he lost his parents in a car crash, five years before. That loss had left a void so deep, he didn't hesitate even for a second when the chance came to become a father. It wasn't just about raising children—it was about rebuilding a family, creating something of his own after fate had so cruelly taken his away.

When the nurse placed Avik and Anika in his arms, something had shifted inside him—something profound, something primal.

They were *his.*

No matter how unprepared he was. No matter how much he had to learn. No matter how impossible it seemed.

They were *his* to protect, to care for, to love.

And in that moment, as he held them close, their warmth seeping into his skin, he had made a silent vow—he would *never* regret this.

No matter how hard it got.

And *God, it had been hard.*

The sleepless nights, the endless crying, the sheer exhaustion of juggling business with bottles and diapers and doctor's appointments. The terrifying realization that *no one*—not money, not power, not connections—could prepare him for the sheer responsibility of keeping two tiny humans alive.

He made mistakes. Plenty of them.

But never—not once—did he question his decision.

Because every time Anika had curled up against his chest, safe and trusting...

Every time Avik had clung to his hand, looking up at him like he was *everything...*

Every time he had seen the love and trust in their eyes...

He had *known.*

He had never made a better choice in his life.

But the life he had built in New York—the life that had once felt invincible—no longer felt right. No longer felt *enough.*

He had spent years growing his empire there, cementing his name in an industry that thrived on power and influence. Yet, for all its successes, for all its luxuries, that city had never been a *home.* Not for him. And certainly not for *them.*

His children deserved more than high-rise apartments and a revolving door of caretakers. They deserved to grow up in a place where values weren't measured in dollar signs, where family still meant something deeper than just a shared last name.

They deserved the kind of childhood *he* had once had.

His parents had given him a home filled with love, with warmth, with traditions that had anchored him even when life got chaotic. He had lost them too soon—but their memories, their legacy, had always stayed with him.

And it was that legacy he wanted to pass on to his children.

So, he had made another choice.

He spent years restructuring his business, moving his base of operations, ensuring that his empire wouldn't just survive the shift—it would *thrive* in it. He had uprooted everything, packed up the life he once thought was unshakable, and finally brought his children *home.*

To India.

To the roots that had shaped him, to the values he wanted them to grow up with.

For *them.*

For his children.

And now, someone had stepped into their lives—so seamlessly, so unexpectedly—that it made his chest ache.

Reva Khanna.

He downed the rest of his whiskey, setting the glass down with more force than necessary.

He couldn't go there.

Wouldn't go there.

Because Reva wasn't just a woman who intrigued him.

She was dangerous.

And Angad Sareen never played a game he wasn't certain he could win.

***

CHAPTER ELEVEN

MORNING AFTER

Reva Khanna: *Good morning. How's Anika feeling today?*

She sent the text before she could overthink it, still curled up in bed, the morning sun filtering through her sheer curtains. The three dots appeared almost instantly.

Angad Sareen: *Better. Fever's gone. She's getting ready for school because she missed her friends yesterday.*

Reva smiled. That was a good sign.

Reva Khanna: *That's great! Kids bounce back fast.*

Angad Sareen: *I just hope she doesn't overexert herself and fall sick again.*

Reva Khanna: *She won't. Kids are more resilient than we think.*

A pause. Then another text.

Angad Sareen: *You seem to know a lot about kids.*

Reva Khanna: *I have a niece, remember?*

Another pause. She could almost picture him smiling.

Reva Khanna: *I have a meeting at the school today. If it's okay with you, I can check on her while I'm there?*

Angad Sareen: *I'd appreciate that. Thank you.*

She smiled, tossing her phone aside as she got out of bed, already thinking about seeing the kids.

*

Angad wasn't expecting a message from Reva first thing in the morning.

When his phone buzzed, he was in the middle of his morning coffee, watching the twins finish their breakfast—Avik grumbling about his toast not being crispy enough, Anika still a little sluggish from the fever. He had just checked her temperature again—normal, but he was still wary.

And then—

Reva Khanna: *Good morning. How's Anika feeling today?*

For a moment, he simply stared at the screen. It was such a small thing—a text, a casual check-in—but it threw him.

He should have expected it. She had been worried last night. She had stayed late. Still, he wasn't used to someone outside of his immediate world—his home, his business—checking in like this.

His fingers hovered over the keyboard for a second before he responded.

Angad Sareen: *Better. Fever's gone. She's getting ready for school because she missed her friends yesterday.*

Reva's reply came quickly.

Reva Khanna: *That's great! Kids bounce back fast.*

He exhaled, his grip on the coffee mug relaxing just a little. But the worry still gnawed at him.

Angad Sareen: *I just hope she doesn't overexert herself and fall sick again.*

He could already picture Anika running around the playground, forgetting that she'd been sick just yesterday.

Reva Khanna: *She won't. Kids are more resilient than we think.*

A small pause.

He found himself smiling, shaking his head as he typed.

Angad Sareen: *You seem to know a lot about kids.*

The reply came almost instantly.

Reva Khanna: *I have a niece, remember?*

He did. She had mentioned Sanaya before, in passing. But it was more than that. She had been at ease with his kids. She had known exactly how to comfort Anika, how to speak to Avik, how to make them feel safe.

Before he could linger on that thought, another text popped up.

Reva Khanna: *I have a meeting at the school today. If it's okay with you, I can check on her while I'm there?*

He didn't hesitate this time.

Angad Sareen: *I'd appreciate that. Thank you.*

And just like that, the knot of worry in his chest loosened a little more.

*

The school corridors always felt familiar, yet distant, a relic of her past. Today, though, they carried an unexpected excitement.

When she entered the principal's office, her aunt, Meera, greeted her with a warm hug.

"You're looking well, *beta*. Though I must say, there's a certain glow about you today."

Reva rolled her eyes. "It's called morning sunlight, *Bua*."

Meera laughed. "Sit, sit. Have some tea before the meeting."

As they settled in, Meera suddenly said, "Did you hear about what happened the other day? One of the newer parents, Mr. Angad Sareen, stormed in, demanding to know about someone named 'Riddhi.' He was furious—accusing us of a security breach, questioning how a stranger could be interacting with his kids on school grounds."

Reva froze, nearly choking on her tea. "Oh God."

Meera raised a brow, her eyes briefly clouded with concern. "We're still looking into it, but we haven't found anyone by that name. There's no log entry, no footage—nothing. It's worrying, security-wise. And if Mr. Sareen storms back in demanding answers, it won't reflect well on the school either."

Reva groaned, setting her cup down.

Meera exhaled, shaking her head. "I've dealt with many protective parents, but the way he reacted… it was too much. Almost excessive."

Without thinking, Reva blurted, "That's because he's a single parent."

Meera's eyes snapped to hers, surprise clear on her face. "How do you know that?"

Reva hesitated for half a second before sighing. "Because I know him. I… I'm… Riddhi."

Meera's eyebrows shot up. "You, what!?!"

"Oh, well, it's all a big misunderstanding. The kids heard Trisha calling me "Ree Di" in school the other day, and they thought my name was *"Reedi."* Because of their accent, their nanny assumed I was "*Riddhi*," and that's how the name got stuck." Reva waved a hand as if that explained everything. "And don't worry about him or the school's reputation. The misunderstanding was cleared last night."

"Last night?" Meera pounced on the slip, her gaze turning sharp with curiosity.

Reva mentally kicked herself. Of course, her aunt wouldn't miss that. "It's not what you think," she rushed to explain. "I'm working with him on a project. We had a business meeting at his home because Anika wasn't well, and I… ended up meeting the kids there." She quickly added, "There were other people there for the meeting, too." But she conveniently left out the part where she stayed back for dinner with him and the kids.

Meera leaned back, an amused smile tugging at her lips. "Hmm. Interesting. Single, you said?"

Reva rolled her eyes. "Yes, he's a single dad," she said, then added pointedly, "And don't read too much into nothing."

Meera's eyes twinkled with mischief. "Ah, I see. And this Angad Sareen… what's he like?"

Reva tried to be nonchalant. "He's… a good father."

Meera gave her a knowing look. "That's not what I asked."

Reva huffed. "He's just… different from what I expected."

"Different, how?"

Reva hesitated, then shook her head. "It doesn't matter."

Meera grinned. "Of course, it doesn't."

Reva pointedly ignored her and checked her watch. "I should head to the boardroom now."

Meera chuckled. "Go on, then. But this conversation isn't over."

*

By the time the school day ended, Reva found herself at the main gates, waiting for Anika and Avik. When they spotted her, their faces lit up.

"Reedi!" Anika threw her arms around Reva's waist, and Avik followed suit.

She hugged them back. "Hey, you two! How was school?"

Anika beamed. "So fun!"

Reva crouched to Anika's level, brushing a stray lock of hair from her forehead. "How are you feeling, sweetheart? Are you tired? Does anything hurt?"

Anika tilted her head as if considering the question, but before she could reply, Avik—always the quicker one to speak—cut in with a solemn expression.

"She's fine," he declared with the confidence of a doctor making a diagnosis. Then, as if revealing a great secret, he added, "I think Anika fell sick because Daddy told us not to meet you."

Reva's breath hitched, her heart clenching at the sheer conviction in his voice. "Oh, Avik…"

"But now all is good," he added firmly.

Before she could respond, Lata appeared, ready to take them home. But the twins had other ideas.

"Can we go with you today, Reedi?" Anika asked, her big hazel-green eyes pleading.

Reva hesitated. "I should ask your dad first."

She quickly texted Angad: *Anika is doing fine. The kids want to come with me. Is that okay?*

Angad's response was almost immediate.

Angad Sareen: *Where to?*

Reva Khanna: *Home.*

Angad Sareen: *What about your work?*

Reva Khanna: *Nothing I can't manage.*

A long pause. Then—

Angad Sareen: *Okay. Just keep me posted.*

She smiled at the kids. "Alright, let's go."

*

Angad's phone buzzed just as he was reviewing a contract, pulling his attention away.

Reva Khanna: *Anika is doing fine. The kids want to come with me. Is that okay?*

His grip on the phone tightened instinctively. His first thought was refusal. They had a routine, a structure. Letting them go off with someone—even Reva—wasn't something he took lightly.

He exhaled sharply and typed back.

Angad Sareen: *Where to?*

The reply came quickly.

Reva Khanna: *Home.*

Home? Hers, not his. He stared at the word for a beat longer than necessary.

Angad Sareen: *What about your work?*

There was no way she wasn't busy. He was familiar with the kind of deadlines she handled. Could she really manage two hyperactive kids on top of everything else?

Reva Khanna: *Nothing I can't manage.*

His jaw flexed. He didn't like decisions that weren't his own, especially ones concerning his children. But they wanted to go. And if he said no, would they feel like he was keeping them from her?

Damn it.

He hesitated longer than he should have before finally typing—

Angad Sareen: *Okay. Just keep me posted.*

He set the phone down, rubbing a hand over his face. He hadn't expected this from her – that she'd care enough to check on Anika at school, that she'd offer to take them home without hesitation. That his kids would already trust her.

And most of all, that he would trust her, too.

***

CHAPTER TWELVE

HOME

As Reva entered her building with the twins, her phone buzzed. Her mother.

"Lunch at home today," her mother said without preamble. "Sanaya has been complaining that she never gets to see her Maasi anymore."

Reva smiled. "Tell her to close her eyes. I have a surprise for her—just two minutes!" She cast a glance at Avik and Anika.

The twins, quick to catch on, giggled and clapped in excitement. "A surprise!" Anika echoed.

When they reached her parents' seventh-floor apartment, the door swung open before Reva could even press the bell. Sanaya stood there, her eyes lit with anticipation.

"*Maasi*! What's the surp—" She wasn't even finished with her question before Avik and Anika stepped into view. Sanaya's delighted squeal filled the hallway.

She grabbed their hands and pulled them inside. "Come, come! Meet my Nanu and Nani!"

Reva's parents, Naina and Rajender 'Raj' Khanna, stood in the living room, watching the exchange unfold.

"Nanu, Nani," Reva said, smiling. "Meet Avik and Anika… my new friends."

Her parents exchanged a glance before warmly welcoming the twins. Her mother's eyes held a silent question, but Reva simply nodded, silently assuring her she'd explain later.

Avik, ever the gentleman, folded his hands in a polite *namaste.* "Namaste, Uncle, Aunty."

Before her parents could respond, Sanaya giggled. "They're not Uncle, Aunty, silly! They're Nanu and Nani!"

Reva's parents chuckled.

"She's right, of course," Raj said, ruffling Avik's hair. "We are Nanu and Nani."

Naina crouched slightly, looking at the kids warmly. "Are you hungry?"

Avik and Anika turned to Reva, waiting for her cue.

The simple action wasn't lost on her parents. Another silent exchange passed between them—curiosity, questions they were holding back for later. Reva sighed inwardly. She'd explain everything soon enough.

She nodded at the twins. "Go on, tell Nani."

Anika hesitated for a second before nodding eagerly. "Yes, please!"

Then, as if suddenly remembering something, she turned back to Naina, her tiny brows knitting together in concern. "But... Daddy said we shouldn't take food from strangers."

For a moment, silence stretched in the room. And then, laughter erupted.

Raj let out a hearty chuckle. "That's a good rule, little one. Your dad is very smart."

Avik lifted his chin slightly, pride shining in his eyes. "Yes, he really is."

Naina shook her head, amused. "He is. But we're not strangers, sweetheart."

Raj leaned forward, smiling. "We're Sanaya's grandparents. And since Sanaya is your friend, that makes us family, don't you think?"

Anika considered that for a second, then turned to Avik, who gave a tiny, thoughtful nod as if approving of the logic.

Reva pressed her lips together, stifling a laugh. The way they took everything so seriously was just too endearing.

"Well..." Anika said slowly, looking back at Naina. "Okay, then. We can eat."

The adults laughed again, and Reva felt a rush of warmth. The way her parents handled the moment—gentle, reassuring, never letting the kids feel awkward—made her love and admire them even more.

Her mother smiled. "Good. We're having *rajma-chawal.* Sanaya loves it, so that's what's for lunch today. Is that okay?"

Anika hesitated. "I've never had *rajma-chawal* before... so I don't know if I like it."

Raj chuckled. “I’m sure you’ll love it. All kids do.”

And sure enough, the meal was a hit. The kids devoured the food, and Avik, ever so composed, turned to Reva mid-bite.

“Can you please teach Raju Bhaiya to make this for us?”

The question seemed harmless enough, but Reva noticed how her mother’s hand stilled as she was about to take another bite.

“Raju Bhaiya?” Naina asked.

Anika answered between bites. “Raju Bhaiya cooks food at our home.”

Naina’s gaze softened, but she probed further. “And your mummy? She doesn’t cook for you?”

Reva stilled.

This time, it was Anika who answered, her voice quieter, tinged with sadness. “We don’t have a mother.”

Reva felt something tighten in her chest. There was something about the way they said it—rehearsed, automatic, as if they had learned to remind themselves, or perhaps others, that their father was enough. That they didn’t need to be asked about what—or who—was missing.

She felt the weight of those words settle around the table, their quiet finality pressing against her ribs. Her parents’ gazes snapped to her, unspoken questions swirling in their eyes. But Reva barely noticed. All she saw were the two small faces before her—one filled with quiet sadness, the other carefully blank, as if bracing for the inevitable reaction.

And it broke her heart.

Reva’s parents shared a glance, an unspoken understanding passing between them. Then Raj, his voice warm and reassuring, steered the conversation to safer ground.

“Well then,” he said with a smile, “I can guarantee your Raju Bhaiya won’t be able to make *rajma-chawal* quite like Nani’s. So anytime you’re craving it, just come here.”

The twins beamed, and Reva felt her heart squeeze.

Her parents didn’t pry further, didn’t react with pity or unnecessary questions. Instead, they simply welcomed the children with the same warmth they had for Sanaya.

Reva smiled at them, silently grateful.

After lunch, with a promise of ice cream later, Reva ushered the kids toward Sanaya’s room to play. Once they were out of earshot, she sat her parents down in the living room.

Taking a deep breath, she told them everything.

How she met the kids at school. Then, at the clubhouse. And how, last evening, she'd gone to a business meeting at her new client, Angad Sareen's home—only to realize that Avik and Anika were his children.

Her mother raised an eyebrow. "So, you were at his place last evening?"

Reva sighed. She should have known they'd catch that detail.

"Ramesh told us he dropped you at Building 9," her mother added. "We weren't sure who you knew there."

"I wasn't alone," Reva clarified. "The whole business team was there. The meeting was held at his home because Anika wasn't well."

Her father leaned back, his expression thoughtful. "Angad Sareen… Any relation to Omkar Sareen?"

Reva blinked. "They moved here from New York, and I have no idea about his family."

Her mother, however, had her own questions, ones that cut straight to the heart of what Reva had been wondering since the moment she first realized whose children Anika and Avik were. "And their mother? Where is she? Is he divorced? Is she…?"

She trailed off, leaving the unspoken question hanging.

Reva didn't have an answer.

Because she didn't know.

And that unsettled her more than it should have.

*

Reva was curled up on her couch, laptop balanced on her knees, fingers flying over the keyboard as she tackled some last-minute work. The apartment was blissfully quiet, allowing her to focus without distractions. With the kids still at her parents' place, happily immersed in Sanaya's toy-filled room, she had hoped to make the most of her time—wrapping up her pending tasks before they inevitably came bursting in, ready for their promised ice cream outing.

The doorbell rang, and without looking up, she smiled, already picturing three eager little faces on the other side. Closing her laptop, she set it aside on the study table before heading to the door.

"Yes, yes… we're going for that ice cream—" Her voice faltered as she pulled the door open.

It wasn't the kids.

It was Angad.

For a moment, she just stared, thrown off by his presence. Dressed in a crisp navy-blue shirt, sleeves rolled up to his forearms, and dark trousers, he looked as effortlessly put together as always. Only now, he was standing at *her* doorstep, and she wasn't prepared for it.

Her grip on the doorknob tightened. "How do you know my apartment number?"

He lifted a brow, eyes gleaming with amusement. "And a *hi* to you, too. Ice cream sounds delicious, and are we playing twenty questions at the door, or can I come in?"

Heat crept up her neck. *Great. Rude, much?*

She cleared her throat. "Hi. Please, come in."

She stepped aside, allowing him in.

Angad entered, his gaze sweeping over the space as he took it in.

Reva's apartment was a reflection of her—warm, elegant, and filled with character. Soft lighting cast a golden glow over the cozy living room, where bookshelves lined one wall, filled with well-worn novels and sleek coffee table books. A deep emerald-green sofa sat at the center, adorned with plush cushions, and a throw was carelessly draped over one arm. Against the far wall, a vintage writing desk stood with neatly stacked papers and her laptop. The space was modern yet inviting, exuding quiet sophistication.

He turned back to her, a teasing smirk playing on his lips. "In case you forgot, *you* gave Lata your address to pass along to me."

She narrowed her eyes. "Right. Should've known."

His amusement didn't fade. "So, where are the kids?"

"307," she answered automatically.

The shift was instant. His body tensed, jaw tightening. "Whose apartment is that?" His voice was clipped, laced with quiet protectiveness.

Reva sighed, already seeing the storm brewing in his eyes. "Relax. It's my parents' place."

His frown didn't ease. "And they're there because…?"

"They didn't want to leave Sanaya's room," she explained, crossing her arms. "It's a toy paradise, apparently."

He exhaled, still visibly on edge, but some of the tension drained from his shoulders. Then, after a pause, he asked, "If they live so close, why not just stay with them?"

Reva blinked, caught off guard by the question.

He wasn't the first person to ask—her mother asked it every chance she got. *Why live alone when home was right there?*

She let out a small laugh. "Now you sound like my mom."

His brows lifted, waiting.

Reva sighed. "Honestly? I need my own space. I love them, but living with parents at this age..." She shook her head. "It's different when you grow up and start seeing them as people—not just as 'Mom and Dad.' They have their routines and habits, and I have mine. It's easier this way. I can be close to them, see them whenever I want, but also have my independence."

Angad didn't speak right away, just watched her, something shifting behind his steady gaze. Then he said, more to himself than to her, "Makes sense."

"Are you coming straight from work?" she asked, eyeing his business attire.

"No," he admitted. "I went home first. Only to realize the kids hadn't come back—*at all*." His voice was gruff, carrying an undertone she couldn't decipher.

Something twisted inside her at that—at the fact that the first thing he'd done upon finding them gone was come straight here. His first instinct was to *find them*. And maybe... to find *her*. Was she reading too much between the lines?

She studied him, something warm settling in her chest.

"And have you had anything to eat?" she asked, echoing the very words he had thrown at her many times before.

His lips curved into a slow, knowing smile. "I wouldn't mind a cup of coffee."

She gestured toward the couch. "Make yourself comfortable," then turned toward the kitchen.

She expected him to head back to the lounge, but instead, she felt him following her. Pausing, she turned around, raising an eyebrow.

He grinned. "I'm comfortable here."

She smiled, shaking her head in amusement as she retrieved the kettle from the cabinet.

"You don't have staff?" he asked, sounding surprised as he leaned against the counter.

She filled the kettle, shrugging. "I live alone. I usually have dinner downstairs with my parents, so I don't really need anyone here. A cleaning lady comes during the day, but that's about it."

Angad was silent for a beat. Then, his voice dropped just a fraction. "So, you mean to say... there's no one around. Just you and me?"

The air in the kitchen *shifted.*

Reva stilled, fingers tightening around the spoon she was holding. She turned, meeting his gaze. The way he was looking at her—intensely, unwaveringly—made her stomach dip.

There was something in his eyes.

Something heated.

Something dangerous.

She swallowed, feeling the charged energy between them like a live wire. They had spent time together before, had spoken in private, but never truly alone. In his office, the staff was just outside the door. The café had been a public space. At his home—his bedroom, even, the kids were present—there had always been someone or something grounding the moment. But this... this was different. She was suddenly hyper-aware of the fact that this was the first time they were completely alone. No kids. No work distractions. Just the two of them, in the quiet of her home.

She wasn't sure who moved first, but they were suddenly closer, the space between them thinning. Her pulse quickened, breath catching as his gaze dropped briefly to her lips, and then back up, darker now.

The kettle whistled, sharp and loud, shattering the moment.

Reva blinked, stepping back as if snapping out of a trance.

She turned hurriedly to pour the coffee, hoping he couldn't hear the pounding of her heart.

***

CHAPTER THIRTEEN

MEET THE FAMILY

The kettle's sharp whistle shattered the charged silence between them. Reva blinked, a faint breath escaping her as she stepped away, the spell broken. Angad did the same, his fingers curling into a fist before he exhaled and ran a hand through his hair. The moment—whatever it had been—was gone. But the air still thrummed with something unsaid, something unfinished.

Reva turned swiftly, poured the coffee, and set his cup on the counter with deliberate care—ensuring no accidental touch. Clearing her throat, she said, "Here you go."

Before he could respond, the doorbell rang.

Her eyes lingered on Angad for a moment too long before she pulled herself away and rushed to the door. "Coming," she called out as she reached for the handle. "Guess who's here…"

The words died on her lips as the door swung open, revealing not just the kids but her father as well, standing behind them.

"Your mother and I need to get ready for dinner with the Sharmas…" Raj began, but his words trailed off as his gaze landed on Angad, who had just stepped out of the kitchen, coffee mug in hand.

Reva stiffened. Her eyes flicked between her father and Angad, heat creeping up her neck. Raj's expression shifted, curiosity flickering in his eyes as he took in the man standing in his daughter's apartment.

Reva's stomach twisted. This was awkward.

She cleared her throat, stepping aside. "Papa, this is Angad… Sareen. Avik and Anika's father. He—uh—he came to pick them up."

Before anything more could be said, the twins bounded toward Angad with squeals of "Daddy!" echoing through the room. Angad, caught mid-sip, quickly set his coffee mug on the nearest side table and crouched just in time to catch both of them in his arms. He let out a soft laugh, burying his face in their messy hair, holding them like he hadn't seen them in weeks instead of hours.

Raj's brows lifted slightly, his expression hard to read. But there was something—an almost imperceptible softening in his eyes as he watched the embrace. He didn't miss the ease with which the children clung to Angad, or how instinctively Angad held them, grounding them with quiet steadiness.

When Angad finally stood up, a twin on either side, Raj's gaze met his. He studied him for a long moment. Not with suspicion, but with quiet assessment.

The weight of that look was heavier than any boardroom stare-down Angad had ever faced. He straightened his shoulders instinctively and offered a small, respectful nod.

He then stepped forward and extended his hand to him, but Raj's next words stopped him.

"You're Omi's son, aren't you?"

Angad's brows knit together in confusion. "I—yes... Did you know him?"

Raj didn't hesitate. Instead of shaking Angad's hand, he grasped it and pulled him into a firm hug. "You look just like him, son."

Angad stiffened, momentarily stunned, before he hesitantly returned the hug. Over Raj's shoulder, his bewildered gaze met Reva's. His eyes questioned hers—*What's going on?*

Reva, just as shocked and clueless, could only shake her head. She had no idea either.

Raj exhaled slowly, his expression easing as he looked at Angad.

"Your parents—Omkar and Renuka—were dear friends of ours," he said, a touch of nostalgia coloring his voice. "You were already overseas by the time Naina and I met Omi and Renu at a friend's gathering. We connected instantly, and from that night on, the four of us were practically inseparable at every social event."

He turned to Reva. "Do you remember meeting them when they came over for dinner just before you left for the U.S. for your studies? You must've been about seventeen or eighteen at the time."

Reva frowned, searching her memories. A vague image of a warm, welcoming couple surfaced—laughter, a beautifully set dinner table, voices overlapping in animated conversation. But she had been too young, too preoccupied with her own things, to truly register their significance in her parents' lives.

Raj's expression shifted as he looked between Reva and Angad as if recalling something long buried. His eyes misted over for a fleeting moment before he shook it off, saying nothing more.

Then, exhaling deeply, he added, "When they passed away in that accident… we weren't in India. We were visiting Reva in the U.S., and by the time we returned, you had already left. We didn't have your number—we never needed it. We thought we had our whole lives ahead of us to get to know you, son."

He shook his head, regret etched into his features. "If there's one thing Naina and I have always regretted, it's not getting to know you." A soft smile touched his lips. "But I suppose it was destined… and here we are."

Angad stood frozen, his mind racing. "You… you're Rajender Khanna?" His voice was barely above a whisper. "Mummy-Papa used to tell me about you over our phone calls… You knew them… you… them… Oh my God."

A rush of emotion overwhelmed him. Without a second thought, he bent down to touch Raj's feet.

Raj immediately pulled him up and into another tight embrace, his voice thick with emotion. "*Beta.*"

And then, as if remembering something urgent, he pulled back and reached for his phone. "Naina. You need to come up here. Now."

*

The elevator chimed, and within seconds, the doors slid open. Out rushed Naina—midway through her makeup, hair still in rollers, a satin robe thrown haphazardly over her blouse and petticoat. The sight would have been comical if not for the sheer panic on her face.

"What? What happened? Is Reva okay? Sanaya? Avik and Anika?" She clutched Raj's arm, eyes wild as she scanned the room. "Raj, are you okay?"

Her voice rose with each question, her alarm evident. Then she stopped abruptly, realizing that everyone was just… standing there. Staring at her.

For a moment, there was silence. Then, like a dam breaking, the kids burst into laughter.

Sanaya clutched her stomach, giggling uncontrollably. "Nani, you look so funny!"

Avik and Anika weren't far behind, pointing at her hair rollers, their little bodies shaking with mirth.

Reva pressed a hand over her mouth, but it was useless—her shoulders started shaking, and then Raj, too, let out an amused chuckle.

Even Angad, who had been caught in the middle of this unexpected family chaos, was struggling to keep a straight face.

Naina, however, was not amused.

Her glare snapped to her husband. "Will someone tell me what the hell was so urgent?" she demanded. "What happened?"

Raj, suddenly looking sheepish, raised his hands in surrender. "Calm down, Naina. We're all fine."

She narrowed her eyes at him, arms crossed, still fuming.

Raj hesitated, then gently turned her toward Angad. "Naina, meet Angad."

Naina's anger didn't fade. In fact, she looked even more exasperated. "Raj, I could have—" She gestured wildly at her state of disarray. "You should have—" Her words stumbled over themselves, frustration rendering her momentarily speechless.

Then, turning to Angad, she sighed, attempting to gather herself. "Sorry, *beta*, but my husband didn't exactly give me time to meet you properly." She shot Raj a withering look before refocusing on Angad.

Raj exhaled slowly, then spoke again, his voice gentler this time. "Naina… this is Angad Sareen." He paused, letting it sink in. "Avik and Anika's father." Another pause. "And Omi and Renu's son."

Silence.

Naina's eyes shifted from Angad to Raj, then back again. Her lips parted as if she were about to speak, but no words came.

"Angad…?" she finally whispered. "Renu's son, Angad? *Our* Angad?"

Raj nodded at every question.

Reva glanced at Angad, who met her gaze briefly before turning back to Naina. The kids, sensing something significant but not quite understanding, looked from one adult to the other, brows furrowed in confusion.

Then, slowly, Angad stepped forward. Without hesitation, he bent down to touch Naina's feet.

Just like her husband, she didn't let him. Instead, she pulled him into a tight embrace.

Angad stiffened for a fraction of a second before his arms came around her. The warmth, the familiarity, the weight of a connection he thought he had lost—it hit him all at once.

Ever since his parents' fatal accident over a decade ago, he'd gone through the motions. He had known responsibility, devotion, and love—but this… this felt like home.

Like family.

*

Anika was the first to break the silence, her little face scrunched up in confusion as she looked between her father and Naina.

"Daddy… what happened? Why is Nani crying? Is she angry at you?"

Angad was too stunned at hearing '*Nani*' to respond—the word—so foreign yet so familiar—lodged itself somewhere deep in his chest.

Before he could find his voice, Naina quickly wiped her tears and smiled at Anika. "No, *bachche*… I'm not angry at all. In fact, I'm very, very happy to meet your daddy." She cupped Anika's cheek, her voice thick with emotion. "These are happy tears."

Sanaya clung to Reva's hand, her face etched with confusion. Avik moved closer, his small hand finding Angad's without a word. He didn't speak—just stood beside him, a quiet pillar of comfort.

Angad looked down at his son and smiled, giving his hand a gentle squeeze.

Reva cleared her throat, breaking the moment. "Uh, Maa… don't you and Papa have to attend a dinner?"

Naina gasped. "Oh my God, yes!" She turned to Raj, her face a mix of emotions—joy, disbelief, and now, a mild sense of panic. "We're getting so late!"

Then, as if just remembering something, she turned back to Angad. "*Beta*, you must come over tomorrow for dinner… if you're free!"

Raj immediately nodded in agreement. "Yes, son, you must. We'll have a drink together in your dad's memory."

Angad hesitated for only a second before nodding. "I'd like that."

Naina patted his cheek, her warmth undeniable, before reluctantly pulling away.

With one last look at Angad, Raj and Naina finally left, hurrying toward the elevator.

The door clicked shut.

And just like that, it was the five of them—three kids, Angad, and Reva—still standing at the entrance, absorbing everything that had just happened.

***

CHAPTER FOURTEEN

REVELATION

It was Reva who broke the silence, forcing a cheer into her voice as she ushered the kids inside. "Who's hungry for a pizza party?"

The three little ones erupted in cheers, all thoughts of the previous moment forgotten in the excitement of food.

Sanaya gasped. "*Maasi*! Ice cream?"

Reva shot her a mock-serious look. "If you all behave well, then ice cream after pizza."

The promise did the trick. The kids rushed to the sofa, bouncing onto the cushions as Reva placed an order with the clubhouse restaurant for pizzas to be delivered to the apartment. While waiting, she made sure they were settled—handing each a glass of milk and putting on a cartoon movie they all liked. Soon, they were engrossed, giggling at the screen, oblivious to everything else around them.

She turned then, eyes searching for Angad—finding him outside on the balcony. He stood with his hands on the railing, looking down at the swimming pool, the play area, and the lush gardens of the complex. From this height, he could see his own penthouse across the expanse, its lights glowing warmly against the night.

She grabbed two glasses and walked over, nudging his arm slightly as she handed one to him. He took it absently, sipping without thought—then stopped, glancing at her. "Gin?"

Reva leaned against the railing beside him. "Well, I figured you could use something stronger than coffee right now… but I don't have whiskey here."

"Gin, then," he said quietly, taking a sip. "I needed this."

She clinked her glass lightly against his. "Here's to family."

Angad let out a breath, a shadow of emotion passing through his gaze as he murmured, "To family."

She studied him for a moment. "Are you okay?"

He nodded, but she wasn't convinced.

"Talk to me," she said softly.

His gaze lingered on hers, unsure, as though the words he wanted were stuck somewhere between his chest and throat.

She stepped closer, placing her free hand over his, squeezing lightly—a silent reassurance.

He parted his lips as if about to speak—

But the doorbell rang.

Reva groaned, frustration slipping out before she could stop it. "Fuck."

As soon as the word left her mouth, her eyes widened in horror. She slapped a hand over her lips, panicking, and immediately glanced toward the kids.

They were too lost in their movie to notice.

She let out a relieved breath, turning back—only to find Angad watching her with a wicked glint in his eyes. He leaned in, voice a low murmur against her ear, the warmth of his breath making her shiver.

"Fuck, alright," he whispered, amusement laced in every syllable.

Reva's breath hitched. She turned sharply, staring at him, but he was already striding toward the door.

By the time she recovered from the effect of him being so close to her and reached the living room, he had already paid the delivery guy and was setting the pizza boxes on the table near the sofa and serving the kids a slice each.

She scowled. "It was my turn to pay for dinner."

Angad leaned against the table, a slow smirk playing on his lips. "Oh, was it? See, I figured since you *invited* me for dinner, you'd also *treat* me to dinner." He paused deliberately, watching her reaction. "But don't worry, *Reedi*… I'll let you get the next one."

Reva froze. The way he said Reedi—his voice deep, teasing—sent a warmth rushing through her that had nothing to do with the alcohol. She narrowed her eyes. "Don't call me that."

He chuckled, taking a bite of his pizza. "Oh, I absolutely will."

Reva raised an eyebrow, crossing her arms. "You *do* know that Reedi is short for *Reva Didi*, right?" She tilted her head. "Do you really want to call me that?"

Angad froze for a split second, realization dawning in his eyes. "Wait… *what*?"

"I didn't think so," Reva smirked, crossing her arms.

Angad stared at her, processing, before shaking his head with a dramatic shudder. "Yeah… *no*." He took a deliberate sip of his drink. "That just killed the mood."

Reva laughed, feeling victorious—until he leaned in again, eyes glinting with mischief.

"But see, now I *have* to find something else to call you," he murmured, voice low.

Reva's breath hitched. "Don't bother," she muttered.

Angad just grinned. "Oh, but I *will*."

She huffed, grabbing the plates and napkins to avoid looking at him. If she met his gaze now, she knew she'd only encourage him further.

The kids, meanwhile, were completely unaware of the simmering undercurrent between the adults. They devoured their pizza, chatting animatedly about the movie, barely pausing to breathe between bites.

When dinner was done and the ice creams were polished off, the movie was still running.

"Daddy," Anika piped up, licking the last of her ice cream from her spoon. "Can we stay till the movie finishes? It's Saturday tomorrow… no school!"

Angad didn't need an excuse to stay longer, but his daughter had handed him one on a silver platter.

"Sure," he said easily. Then, glancing at Reva, he added, "We'll be out on the balcony. Call if you need anything."

Reva met his gaze, something unspoken passing between them.

He followed her outside, where the cool night air contrasted with their warm skin. They sat on the patio sofa in comfortable silence, the cool night breeze carrying the distant sounds of the city. Below them, the garden and pool shimmered under soft lights, the faint laughter of children playing in the distance adding to the quiet hum of the evening.

Reva took a sip from her glass, stealing a glance at Angad. His profile was sharp against the glow from the apartment, his jaw tight and his eyes distant. She hesitated before asking, "Do you want to talk?"

Angad turned his head slightly, his gaze meeting hers—longer than he intended. There was something in her eyes, something patient and steady that made him want to say yes. But instead, he exhaled and looked back out at the garden.

Reva understood his silence and didn't push further.

For a while, the only sound between them was the clinking of ice in their glasses. Then, Angad spoke.

"When my parents died, I thought I was all alone in this world." His voice was low, rough around the edges. "Being an only child… There was no one," he said quietly, his voice carrying the weight of old, unspoken loneliness. "No siblings to lean on. No cousins dropping by. After my parents… it was just me."

He paused, a humorless chuckle escaping his lips. "And then Avik and Anika came along. And everything changed. In the space of a heartbeat, I wasn't alone anymore. I had a family. Two tiny, wrinkled, impossibly fragile beings who looked up at me like I was their entire world."

He exhaled, a hand dragging through his hair. "I was terrified. Overwhelmed. But also… for the first time since my parents died, I felt anchored. I had a purpose beyond. I had them. And with that love came this enormous, crushing responsibility—because they depended on me for everything. And I couldn't afford to fail."

Reva listened, saying nothing, just letting him speak.

"I've always wished they had gotten to know their grandparents," he continued, his grip tightening around his glass. "Someone to spoil them. Someone to love them besides me. And if something ever happened to me…" His voice trailed off. He took a steadying breath. "That's always been my biggest fear. What would they do? Who would they have?"

He turned to Reva, something raw and unguarded in his eyes. "And then tonight happened." He let out a shaky breath. "The way your parents opened their hearts to them. The moment Anika called your mom 'Nani'… I… I froze." He shook his head. "I wasn't ready for that."

"I know," Reva murmured. "I noticed."

Angad looked away again, his throat bobbing. "For years, it's just been me and them. The three of us. I never let myself think about… more. Because wanting more—needing more—leads to disappointment."

Reva shifted in her seat, angling toward him. "Not always."

He scoffed, but there was no real bite to it. "You're an optimist."

She smiled softly. "Not always."

He turned to look at her again, his gaze searching hers. The weight of everything unspoken pressed between them—grief, fear, and the unexpected ties that bound their lives together.

After a moment, Reva reached out, her fingers hesitating before settling over his. "You're not alone, Angad."

His fingers curled slightly under hers, not quite holding on but not pulling away either. His Adam's apple bobbed as he swallowed. "It sure feels like it."

Silence.

Reva stood, setting her glass down as she made her way inside to check on the kids. The movie had ended, but they hadn't made it to the end credits. All three of them—Sanaya, Avik, and Anika—were curled up on the sofa, fast asleep. A soft smile tugged at her lips.

Careful not to wake them, she fetched a few blankets, draping them gently over their small bodies. She turned off the TV, dimmed the lights, and took a moment to just watch them—so peaceful, so unaware of the complexities of the world around them. Anika had her fingers curled in the fabric of Avik's shirt as if, even in sleep, she needed to hold onto her brother.

Something tightened in her chest.

She turned, grabbed the bottle from the cabinet, and headed back to the balcony. Angad was still there, staring at nothing, lost in thought. He glanced at her when she returned, wordlessly watching as she refilled their glasses.

Reva hesitated, swirling the liquid in her glass before looking at him. There was something she wanted to ask—something she didn't quite know how to. But when her eyes met his, he seemed to understand.

"Ask," he said, his voice rough but patient.

Encouraged, she took a breath. "Your wife…" She trailed off, searching his face.

To her shock, he exhaled and said, "Never had one."

Her brow furrowed. "What?"

"I mean, not in the way you're thinking." He took a slow sip of his drink, then leaned back in his chair. "I never had a wife, Reva. I've never been married."

Her heart skipped a beat. "Then Avik and Anika…"

"Oh, they're mine, alright," he said, his lips quirking though there was no humor in it.

She stared at him, confused, and he let out a breath, setting his glass down. "Bridgette," he said, the name tasting bitter on his tongue. "That was her name. I was a different man then—driven, careless, lost in the illusion that I could have it all. She was available, eager… and I didn't think twice. One night of indulgence, and just like that, everything changed. I barely knew her. A few weeks later, she showed up, telling me she was pregnant, asking for money… for abortion." His voice hardened. "She didn't want kids. Didn't want to be a mother. But she wanted my money."

Reva felt cold.

"I had a DNA test done to be sure, then made her a deal," he said, his gaze drifting to the night sky. "I told her I'll cover all her medical expenses—everything—if she carries the pregnancy to term. When she found out it was twins, she demanded more money." His jaw tightened. "And the day they were born, she signed them over to me. A clean break. A contract."

Reva sat frozen, absorbing his words. She felt something burning inside her—a fury so intense she didn't know what to do with it. "She just… gave them up?" Her voice trembled with anger. "Like she was a surrogate. Like they meant nothing?"

Angad's jaw clenched. "Not everyone has a heart, Reva," he said quietly, watching her. "Not everyone is like you."

Reva's eyes filled with silent tears, her chest aching for the little boy and girl sleeping inside, for the man who had been carrying all of this alone.

Angad leaned forward, reaching out to wipe away a tear that had escaped down her cheek. His fingers lingered, warm against her skin. Her breath hitched.

The air between them changed—thickened.

She looked at him, really looked at him, and saw something raw in his gaze. Longing. Need.

And then he kissed her.

Slowly at first, as if testing the waters, his lips brushed over hers—soft, warm, intoxicating. She melted into him, her fingers gripping his shirt as he deepened the kiss. His hand slid to the back of her neck, tilting her head just right as he took more, his tongue sweeping against hers in a slow, sensual glide.

A low, desperate sound escaped her throat, and that was all the encouragement he needed. The kiss turned urgent, consuming. His hand splayed across her waist, pulling her closer while her fingers curled into his hair, anchoring herself to him.

The taste of gin lingered between them, but it wasn't the alcohol making her dizzy—it was him. The way he devoured her as if he'd been starving for this. For her.

When they finally broke apart, they were both breathless, foreheads resting against each other.

Reva's pulse pounded. "Angad…"

His fingers traced her jaw, his thumb brushing her swollen lower lip. "I know," he murmured, his voice husky.

But neither of them moved away.

***

CHAPTER FIFTEEN

REFLECTION

As they sat on the patio sofa, the silence stretched between them. Reva remained tucked against Angad's side, her head resting on his shoulder, his arm loosely wrapped around her. Their breathing had slowed, their heartbeats returning to a steady rhythm, but neither moved, as if breaking the moment would shatter something fragile between them.

Then, without warning, Angad shifted. His warmth disappeared as he pulled away and stood up abruptly.

"I need to go," he said, his voice quieter than usual.

Reva blinked, startled. "What about the kids? You don't want to wake them up."

He hesitated, looking torn.

"Let them sleep here," she offered. "I'll send them home in the morning."

A small nod. No argument. No excuses. Just acceptance.

And then he left. Without another word. Without looking back.

Reva exhaled slowly, still feeling the ghost of his lips on hers. Their first kiss… and it had been everything. More than she had ever imagined. His lips had fit against hers like they belonged there, like they were meant to. Like she was meant to.

Her fingers brushed against her lips absentmindedly. The kiss had been hot, urgent, unlike anything she had ever experienced. She had kissed before—Manish had been her only other real kiss—but compared to this, that had been child's play. This… this had been something else entirely.

A kiss that scorched. Consumed.

Nothing like the sweet, tentative kisses of her past. This had been raw, untamed—a collision of need and desperation. The kind of kiss that stole the air from her lungs, making her forget where she was and who she was. The kind that left no room for doubt that she was *wanted.*

For those few breathless moments, there had been no hesitation, no second-guessing. Just the heat of his mouth on hers, the firm grip of his hands, the sheer intensity of it all. He had kissed her like a man starved, like he had been waiting for this—*for her*—for longer than he cared to admit.

And she?

She had melted. Fallen. Given in so completely that it terrified her.

She had wanted more, to touch him, to feel him. When she had whispered his name afterward, he simply said, *I know.*

But then… nothing.

He hadn't touched her again, hadn't pulled her closer, hadn't even looked at her before leaving.

He was gone.

And she was left wondering if it had meant anything at all.

Her stomach twisted.

Did he regret it?

The thought clawed at her, sinking deep, refusing to let go.

Reva squeezed her eyes shut, frustration bubbling beneath the surface. *Stop overthinking.* But she knew herself too well. The moment Angad had walked away without a second glance, doubt had slithered in, whispering cruel possibilities.

Had the kiss been a mistake? A weak moment?

It had been perfect—until it wasn't.

Why?

Because he had come to his senses? Because, in the aftermath, he had realized what he had done.

Reva's chest tightened.

She had been there. *Available. Convenient.* That was all.

Angad could have any woman he wanted. She had seen the way people looked at him. The confidence, the power, the undeniable presence he carried—he could walk into a room and command attention without trying. Women probably lined up for the chance to be with him.

And she was… her.

She had spent years convincing herself she was enough, that she didn't need validation from a man. More so after Manish cheated on her. But right now, the insecurities she had buried so carefully came rushing back, loud and impossible to ignore.

She wasn't the kind of woman someone like Angad Sareen would chase after.

So why had he kissed her?

Because he was vulnerable.

Not because he wanted her, not because she was special. Just because, for a brief moment, he had needed comfort.

And she had just been there.

*

Angad sat on Reva's balcony, his arm still wrapped around her as their breathing slowly returned to normal. Her head rested against his shoulder, her warmth seeping into him, grounding him. But his mind was anything but calm.

That kiss... it had unraveled him.

And that was the problem.

He needed some space.

He exhaled sharply and stood up. "I need to go."

Reva lifted her head, blinking up at him. "What about the kids? You don't want to wake them up."

He hesitated. She was right. Avik and Anika were curled up inside, fast asleep on her couch. The idea of leaving them behind—of not waking them up and taking them home—was foreign to him. He had never spent a night away from them since the day they were born.

But right now, he *needed* to be alone.

Reva must have sensed his turmoil because she spoke gently. "Let them sleep. I'll send them home in the morning."

He nodded, the lump in his throat making it impossible to speak. He turned and walked away, forcing himself *not* to look back.

Because if he did, he might not leave at all.

*

Back in his penthouse, Angad poured himself another drink, stronger this time. His hand gripped the whiskey glass a little too tightly. He took a slow sip, his other hand braced on the edge of the balcony railing as he stared across the garden toward Reva's apartment.

Her balcony lights were off.

She must have gone inside to sleep. In her bed.

A bed he suddenly couldn't stop thinking about.

He closed his eyes, but that only made it worse. All he could see was her mouth beneath his. Her lips, soft and yielding, molded perfectly against his. The way she had kissed him back—not hesitantly, not out of politeness—but with fire, with hunger.

She had wanted him.

Just as desperately as he had wanted her.

But why?

Reva had a heart too big for her own good. Maybe, after learning the truth about Bridgette, she had kissed him because she *pitied* him. Maybe she had seen the broken parts of him and reacted the way she always did—with kindness, with warmth.

And yet, as much as he wanted to believe that, he couldn't shake the way she had melted into him. The way her fingers had fisted in his shirt like she *needed* to hold on to him.

It had been years—longer than he cared to admit—since he had thought about himself. Since he had allowed himself to want, to need. His prime years had been consumed by fatherhood, by ensuring his motherless twins had everything they needed, by making sure they never felt the void their mother had left behind. And he didn't regret a second of it.

But somewhere along the way, he had forgotten what it felt like to crave something just for himself. To lose himself in another person. No woman had enticed him enough—until Reva.

With others, it had always been a surface-level, fleeting attraction at best. A pretty face, a charming smile, but nothing that reached inside him, nothing that made him pause. He had shut that part of himself off for so long, convinced that desire, passion, love—none of it had a place in his life anymore. Not when he had two little hearts depending on him.

But Reva… Reva had slipped through the cracks in his carefully built walls before he even realized it. She challenged him, frustrated him, made him laugh when he least expected it. And now, she consumed his every thought. The way she looked at him, like she saw past his scars, past the weight he carried, straight into the man he had almost forgotten he was.

She had undone him with just a kiss. And that terrified him.

He dragged a hand down his face, exhaling sharply.

None of it mattered.

Reva was perfect. Not just beautiful, but kind, selfless. The way she had opened her home and her heart—not just to him, but to his children. The way her parents had welcomed them had made them feel like family.

But he could never take advantage of that generosity.

Because the truth was, Reva deserved better than a man with baggage.

She wasn't just some woman he could claim because he wanted to. She was her parents' precious daughter, cherished and protected, the kind of woman who deserved the world at her feet. A woman who, one day, would have a family of her own—a husband who could give her everything, children she would carry and love from the moment they were born.

A future with someone unencumbered, someone who could put her first.

Not a man like him. Not a man whose life revolved around two little souls who depended on him for everything.

Reva was warmth, light, and possibility. She could have anyone, build any future she wanted. And he… he was a father before anything else, a man whose priorities had been set in stone the day his twins were born.

She deserved more than the weight of his responsibilities.

And his kids…

They weren't hers.

She loved them, yes. But one day, she would want children of her own. And then what? Where would that leave Avik and Anika?

Angad took another sip of whiskey, the burn doing nothing to dull the ache in his chest.

He had kissed her like a man drowning as if she were the only thing keeping him afloat.

But Reva Khanna was not his to have.

***

CHAPTER SIXTEEN

UNSPOKEN WORDS

As Angad stepped through the door of Raj and Naina's home, the familiar scent of carom seeds and cumin wafted from the kitchen. The clink of crockery, soft laughter—everything felt welcoming. And yet, his gaze scanned the room instinctively, seeking *her*.

But she wasn't there. He could feel it—her absence settled into his chest even before his eyes confirmed it.

A trace of disappointment passed through him. It was strange—after everything that had happened, he'd been dreading this evening. But the hollow feeling of not seeing her was sharper, more unsettling than he'd expected. He told himself it was a relief, but the lie didn't quite settle.

He masked the feeling quickly, offering a warm smile as Raj and Naina came to greet them. He bent down to touch the elders' feet—something he'd grown up doing but had rarely done since moving abroad.

"Bless you, *beta*," Naina said, ruffling his hair in a way only a mother does.

Before Angad could straighten, a small figure moved beside him. Avik bent down, mirroring his father's gesture with solemn reverence, his tiny hands gently touching Raj's and Naina's feet.

For the second time in as many days, Angad froze.

Raj let out a soft chuckle, visibly moved. "Now that's a sight," he said, patting Avik's head as the boy stood proudly.

Misty-eyed, Angad placed a hand on his son's shoulder, swallowing the lump rising in his throat. He'd never taught him to do that. Never asked. Yet, Avik had observed and chosen it himself.

A small moment—but it felt monumental.

Raj looked at him knowingly. "Kids learn more from the actions of their parents than their words," he said, his voice rich with approval. "And you, Angad, are doing a splendid job."

Angad's throat tightened. He managed a nod, brushing a hand down Avik's back.

Then Anika, not one to be left behind, stepped forward and bent down to follow suit—until Naina gently stopped her with a hand on her shoulder.

"No, *beta*," she said kindly. "Girls don't touch feet."

Anika blinked up, confused. "Why not?"

Naina smiled gently. "Have you ever seen your Reedi or Sanaya do it?"

Anika frowned, thinking. "No…"

Crouching down to meet her eyes, Naina brushed a hand over her cheek. "Because daughters of the house are believed to be forms of the Goddess. We honor them—we don't ask them to bow."

Anika's face lit up with awe. "Really?"

"Really," Naina said, kissing her forehead.

Anika beamed. Avik, however, crossed his arms with a frown. "That's not fair."

The room burst into laughter at their completely opposite expressions.

"Come on now," Raj said, ushering them all in. "Let's eat before Naina starts another lecture on traditions, and I end up sleeping hungry."

As they moved toward the dining table, Avik tugged at Naina's hand. "Where's Reedi? She promised she'd be here."

Naina sighed softly. "She had some work, sweetheart."

The kids shared a look of quiet disappointment.

So did Angad.

But before anyone could dwell on it too long, Naina clapped her hands. "Well, let's start dinner—and save a plate for your Reedi. Who knows, she might just surprise us."

And just like that, the evening moved forward—full of warmth, laughter, and the quiet longing for someone who was missed more than she knew.

*

Reva had debated skipping dinner at her parents' place.

Lata came in the morning to pick up the kids. Sanaya also went downstairs, and just like that, the house had gone from chaotic to eerily quiet. The twins were too excited to notice her sudden silence, already buzzing with excitement over their evening with Sanaya.

"See you at Nanu-Nani's place, Reedi!" Anika had called out cheerfully before skipping out the door, Avik right behind her.

They overheard Raj and Naina inviting Angad to dinner the previous night, and by then, their own plans were already set.

And that was precisely why she didn't want to go.

Reva had come up with at least five reasonable excuses to avoid it—work, a last-minute client call, a migraine, or maybe even pretending she had plans with a friend. But none held up against her mother's persistence.

"*Beta*, you barely had time to spend with Sanaya this time, and she's leaving soon. She'll feel bad if you don't come. And even Avik and Anika would be there..."

And just like that, she was trapped.

So here she was, standing at the threshold of a home filled with warmth, laughter, and the unmistakable comfort of family. The smell of home-cooked food wrapped around her like a familiar embrace, and the sound of Avik, Anika, and Sanaya's giggles filled the space as they huddled over a tablet, engrossed in some game.

Her father sat at the dining table with a drink in hand, while Naina moved around, fussing over the food and making sure everyone had enough.

And then there was him.

Angad.

Sitting at the dining table, his broad frame relaxed, one arm resting on the back of his chair as he listened to Raj talk. He hadn't noticed her yet.

But the moment she stepped in, as if sensing her presence, his gaze lifted.

Their eyes met.

A fraction of a second. Barely a beat.

Then, just as quickly, they looked away.

Reva's heart gave a traitorous thump against her ribs.

She forced herself to keep moving, her expression neutral, but the air between them had already shifted. She felt it in the way her skin prickled, in the weight of unsaid words lingering between them.

Dinner was going to be... complicated.

*

Outwardly, everything was normal. The meal was delicious, the conversation flowed, and the kids filled any silence with their chatter. But beneath it, there was tension. A pull that neither Reva nor Angad acknowledged, yet both felt with every breath.

"You know, Angad, I got into investing in real estate much later in life. Back in the day, I was all about finance—number crunching, risk assessments... but life had other plans," Raj said with a chuckle, swirling the drink in his hand. "It wasn't even on my radar until Omi came into the picture. He had an eye for the right properties and knew the ins and outs of the market. He helped me secure a few good deals early on and gave me the confidence to take the plunge. The rest, as they say, is history. He's the one who suggested I invest in Gurugram all those years back... and look where we are now."

Angad's fingers curled tighter around his glass, though his face stayed composed. "Yeah... he had a way of seeing things others didn't. Not just in business—everywhere. He never second-guessed himself."

Raj nodded, a small smile playing on his lips. "That's what set him apart. The confidence, the instinct... It wasn't just luck; it was calculated risk. And damn if he wasn't always right."

Angad let out a quiet exhale, staring into his whiskey. "Yeah. He was."

He could still hear his father's voice, the sharp certainty in it, the way he made decisions without hesitation. Omkar Sareen had built his life on sharp instincts and unshakable conviction. Angad had spent years trying to live up to that name, that legacy.

And yet, tonight, with Reva just a few feet away, he felt anything but certain.

Angad responded at the right moments, kept up with the conversation, but his mind... his mind wasn't here.

It was on her.

He felt her before he saw her. That subtle shift in the air, the barely perceptible pause in movement when she stepped in.

And then, as if drawn by some invisible force, his gaze lifted.

Reva.

She hesitated, just for a second, at the sight of him. Just long enough for him to catch the barest hint of hesitation in her eyes before she recovered and stepped fully into the room. But that one moment was enough. Enough for Angad to feel the tension coil inside him, enough to feel her presence like a tangible force in the air.

Even as Raj kept talking, Angad was excruciatingly aware of her every movement—the way she greeted her mother with a kiss on the cheek, the soft clink of her bangles as she tucked a strand of hair behind her ear, the way she deliberately didn't look at him.

His jaw tightened.

He wasn't the only one avoiding eye contact. Reva did, too. *Did she regret last night?*

He turned back to Raj, forcing himself to focus, to push back the memory of last night—the taste of her, the feel of her pressed against him, the way his name had fallen from her lips in a breathless whisper.

But it was useless.

Because she was right there, not looking at him. Had barely spoken to him. But he could feel her presence—every shift of her posture, every time her fingers brushed her glass. And damn it, every time she laughed, the sound went straight to his chest like a punch he hadn't braced for.

No matter how much distance he tried to put between them, there wasn't a damn thing he could do to stop wanting her.

*

Reva focused too hard on her plate, cutting her food into tiny, unnecessary pieces. Angad, on the other hand, seemed engrossed in his *dal*, eating with the precision of a man determined to avoid unnecessary conversation.

"Reva, Angad was just telling us about his new project. The one you are both working on together. Isn't that exciting?" Naina asked, smiling warmly.

Reva forced herself to nod, her voice coming out too polite, too neutral. "Yeah, it's great."

Angad didn't respond immediately, but Reva noticed the way his shoulders tensed.

The tension wasn't lost on her parents either. Though they said nothing, she could feel their curious glances—especially her mother's—as if she was piecing together a puzzle.

Thankfully, the kids, oblivious to the charged atmosphere, chattered on.

"Reedi made us pancakes today for breakfast!" Avik suddenly announced, breaking the silence. "And they were way better than Raju Bhaiya's!"

Anika nodded enthusiastically. "Yeah, hers were soft and fluffy. Raju Bhaiya always burns them a little."

Avik smirked. "That's because he tries too hard to make them 'American-style.'"

Sanaya giggled.

Angad stiffened for a second before clearing his throat. "That's nice, buddy." His voice was even, but there was something in his expression—something unreadable, guarded.

Reva felt a strange twist in her stomach.

She wasn't even sure why.

*

Dinner dragged on, the underlying tension never quite dissolving. Once the plates were cleared, everyone moved to the living room, settling in with their drinks. Reva chose not to drink; instead, she kept herself occupied with the kids, playing a board game with them while the adults talked.

Angad, still feeling the weight of the evening, was just about ready to leave when Raj and Naina shared an unexpected update.

"So, there's a slight change of plans," Raj said, setting down his glass. "Rohini and Sumit won't be able to come to pick up Sanaya. Their work trip got extended."

Naina nodded. "Which means we're leaving for Mumbai next Sunday to drop her off. We'll stay for a few days, probably a week, until they return."

The reaction was instant.

"What?!" Anika's face fell. "Why does she have to go?"

"Yeah, why can't she just stay here?" Avik added, his brows furrowed.

Sanaya sighed. "I wish I could, but my school is starting, so I need to be there."

The twins sulked, clearly unhappy with the news. Then, as if a light bulb switched on, Sanaya perked up. "Hey! What if you guys come with us to Mumbai?"

Both Avik and Anika turned to the older couple with hopeful eyes.

"Can we, Nanu? Nani?" Anika pleaded.

Naina glanced at Raj, exchanging a thoughtful look before smiling. "That's actually a good idea. Why don't we take them with us? It'll be a fun little trip, and we'll bring them back in a week."

All three kids gasped in excitement before turning to the only person whose approval truly mattered.

Angad.

Six eager eyes locked onto him, waiting for his answer.

Reva found herself holding her breath.

Angad leaned back, his expression giving nothing away. He had never spent a single night away from his kids—until last night, and even that had been an aberration, driven by a moment he still hadn't fully processed. The thought of being apart from them for days gnawed at him in a way he couldn't quite put into words. Could he do it?

Could he let go—just this once?

Raj put his hand on Angad's shoulder in understanding. "Son, it's time you let the grandparents spoil them properly. Trust us."

Naina nodded, running a soothing hand over Anika's hair. "You've done an incredible job raising them, Angad, but they need this. A little adventure. A break from routine. And so do you."

"I don't need a break." His voice was firm, but there was hesitation in his eyes.

Reva, sitting quietly on the couch, didn't say a word. She didn't push, didn't nudge him in any direction. It had to be his decision.

Raj chuckled, shaking his head. "Of course you do. You just don't realize it yet." He gave Angad a knowing look. "They'll be in good hands. Let them go, *beta*. You can send their nanny along if you like."

Angad's eyes landed on the twins. Anika was staring up at him with pleading eyes. Avik was trying to act neutral, but he clutched Raj's hand a little too tightly.

A week.

Could he do it? Could they?

Finally, he sighed, rubbing a hand down his face. "You'll call me every day?"

"Twice a day!" Anika promised.

"Video call!" Avik added.

"Okay," he muttered, almost to himself. "Okay."

The kids cheered. Naina beamed. Raj patted Angad's back again. And Reva—still silent—watched Angad carefully.

Because she knew he wasn't just letting go of his kids for a week, he was learning to let go of control.

And that was a start.

***

CHAPTER SEVENTEEN

UNCHARTED TERRITORY

It had been a whirlwind week of last-minute shopping and packing—clothes, books, toys—all the while coordinating with school authorities to inform them about the upcoming absence.

On the day of their departure, the kids were packed and ready, their excitement barely contained as they huddled together. Their small suitcases stood lined up by the door, and Lata fussed over their travel essentials, double-checking everything even though Angad had already done the same.

He and the kids arrived at the building entrance along with Lata, who was also accompanying them to Mumbai to look after them. Raj, Naina, and Reva were already waiting in the car. The twins chattered excitedly, their voices a mix of anticipation and impatience. Their tiny hands fidgeted with their backpacks, sneakers tapping against the pavement as they bounced on their feet.

The moment Reva stepped outside, they spotted her.

"Reedi!" Anika squealed, breaking into a sprint. Avik followed right behind her, both of them colliding into Reva with tight, eager hugs.

Laughing, she crouched down to their level, smoothing Anika's hair and squeezing Avik's shoulder. "Excited for your big trip?"

"Super excited!" Avik grinned. "But we were waiting for you."

Then came the inevitable request.

"Reedi, come with us in Daddy's car!" Anika insisted, gripping her arm.

"Yes, yes! You and Sanaya both!" Avik chimed in, bouncing on his heels. "Lata Aunty can go with Nanu-Nani in the other car."

Reva hesitated, her eyes darting toward Angad, who had remained silent so far. For a moment, something shadowed his expression—annoyance, maybe, or reluctance—gone before she could be certain. But under the hopeful gazes of the kids, saying no wasn't an option.

Before she could come up with a response, Raj chuckled. "Go with them, Reva. Never say no to kids." He turned to Ramesh, the driver. "Help Angad with the luggage, and make sure Lata sits with us."

Lata nodded, already moving toward the other car as the twins tugged on Reva's hands.

"Please, Reedi?" Anika pleaded, eyes wide.

With a soft sigh and a reluctant smile, Reva gave in. "Alright, alright. I'm coming."

The kids cheered, climbing into the back seat while Reva moved toward the passenger side of Angad's car, feeling an odd tension in her limbs. She hadn't seen him since the dinner at her parents' place the week before, and the distance—intentional or not—hung between them like unspoken air.

She kept her attention on the kids, letting their infectious enthusiasm fill the car as she buckled herself into the passenger seat. The moment they pulled out of the society, Anika started rattling off their plans for Mumbai.

"We'll go to the beach first, right, Sanaya?"

Sanaya nodded eagerly. "Yes! And we have to go to my favorite ice cream place near Marine Drive."

"And the aquarium!" Avik chimed in. "You promised, Sanaya."

Reva smiled, encouraging them as they excitedly mapped out their trip, their voices overlapping in bursts of joy. She nodded along, asked questions, laughed at their antics. Not once did she glance at Angad. Not once did she acknowledge his presence beside her.

And Angad… said nothing either.

He gripped the steering wheel, his eyes fixed on the road ahead, his jaw tight. She wasn't ignoring him—not entirely. But she wasn't engaging with him either. It was as if she had drawn an invisible line, a barrier he wasn't sure how to cross.

But he felt her.

Even as she laughed with the kids, even as her voice remained light and easy, he felt her. The slight shift in her posture when he turned the wheel. The way her fingers curled around the fabric of her dress when his knuckles brushed too close to the gear. The way she never once turned her head, yet she was hyper-aware of him.

And he was aware of her.

Her scent lingered in the space between them—a soft, familiar blend of something floral with a hint of vanilla. The way she tucked her hair behind her ear when Sanaya spoke animatedly, revealing the curve of her neck. The way her lips curved when she teased Anika and how that very same mouth had been tight with hesitation when she agreed to sit in his car.

The silence between them wasn't empty. It wasn't even uncomfortable. It was just there, heavy and charged, stretching through the car like an unspoken challenge.

And neither of them acknowledged it.

*

The moment they reached the departure terminal, the excitement dulled just a little. The twins held onto Angad, their grip tighter than usual.

"You'll call us?" Anika asked, her voice barely above a whisper, uncertainty clouding in her big, hazel-green eyes.

Angad crouched down to her level, brushing a strand of hair from her cheek. "Didn't you say you'd be the one calling me?" he asked gently, his tone playful to ease the tightness in her chest.

Anika's lips curved into a tentative smile. "Every day," she whispered, pinky finger already extended toward his.

"Twice a day," Avik corrected.

Angad chuckled, linking his pinky with both of theirs. "Yes, with extra hugs over the phone."

Sanaya, with her whole extra year of experience over the twins, rolled her eyes. "Guys, you'll survive," which made everyone laugh. But even she lingered in her hug with Angad before stepping back.

Reva watched as Angad cupped Anika's face before pressing a kiss to her forehead, then doing the same for Avik. The kids clung to him, their tiny hands fisting in his jacket, their reluctance now evident.

He wasn't just their father. He was their whole world.

And in that moment, something hit her with quiet force—the depth of his loneliness.

The twins then turned to her, throwing their arms around her in a tight hug. "Reedi, please take care of daddy while we're gone!" Anika whispered, her voice muffled against Reva's shoulder.

Avik nodded seriously. "Promise us, okay?"

Reva stilled for a second, her eyes darting to Angad, who looked just as taken aback as she felt. Her heart stumbled over itself, but she forced a smile, smoothing Avik's hair. "Of course I will," she said softly.

Satisfied, they grinned and hugged her one last time before turning back to Angad, wrapping themselves around him.

Naina stepped forward, her gaze soft as she reached up and touched Angad's cheek, the gesture maternal, reassuring. "They'll be fine," she promised. "I'll make sure they call you. And video call you. As many times as they want."

Angad swallowed and nodded, though the tension in his shoulders remained. For five years, every decision he'd made had revolved around his children—every work trip, every late night, every carefully crafted plan designed to keep him close, never too far.

And now, they were walking away.

Their small hands, slipping from his grasp.

Even if only for a week, it felt like an ache he hadn't prepared for.

"They'll be fine," Naina said again, her voice gentle but firm. "And so will you."

He exhaled, his jaw tightening, but he managed to nod again.

Reva watched the exchange, a strange mix of emotions stirring inside her. She wasn't sure why the sight of Naina comforting Angad unsettled her, but it did. Maybe because she had never really thought about what it meant for him to be so alone. To be the only one responsible for two little hearts that loved him more than anything in the world.

A final round of hugs, a flurry of goodbyes, and then the kids were gone—little backpacks bouncing as they walked toward security, their hands tucked into Naina and Raj's.

Angad stood still, hands shoved into his pockets, his gaze fixed on them until they disappeared past the checkpoint. Only then did he release a breath, one that seemed to take something out of him.

Reva exhaled softly and turned to Ramesh. "You can head back home. I'll come with Angad Sir."

That made Angad turn. His brows furrowed slightly.

"You don't have to," he said, voice low.

"Unless you have some plans...?" she added, suddenly unsure. Maybe he did. Maybe he had been waiting for this—some long-overdue time for himself.

Angad met her gaze. Then, after a long beat, he murmured, "No, Reva. For the first time in five years, I have absolutely no plans. I don't even know what to do."

Something in Reva's chest pulled tight.

On instinct, she reached out and squeezed his arm—just a brief press of her fingers, but enough to ground him. To tell him he wasn't as alone as he thought.

"Then," she said lightly, "let me take you out for dinner."

*

The car ride was quiet at first, the space between them heavy with something unspoken. Reva tapped her fingers against her knee, glancing sideways at him. Angad's face was impassive, his gaze fixed on the road, but she could see the tension in his jaw, the way his fingers gripped the steering wheel just a little too tightly.

She cleared her throat. "We could go to a restaurant, or I could cook at home—whichever you prefer."

Angad's grip tightened further. "No," he said, too quickly. "Home's not a good idea."

Reva stiffened.

The rejection was immediate, decisive.

Of course, it wasn't a good idea.

Memories of the last time they had been alone together flashed through her mind—his mouth on hers, his hands in her hair, the way her body had melted against his.

She should have known better than to even suggest it.

He didn't want to be alone with her.

And she was done chasing after men who didn't want her.

Forcing herself to act unaffected, she let out a small hum. "Okay. There's a new place I've been meaning to try. Lovely terrace seating, great Asian food."

Angad nodded, his gaze never wavering from the road. "Fine by me."

Anything, as long as it meant he wouldn't be alone with her.

Because God help him, he didn't trust himself around her. Not after last time. Not after the way she had felt in his arms, warm and soft and so damn right. He had barely managed to pull himself away then. What made him think he could do it again?

For five years, he had never let himself slip. Never allowed himself to even *think* of something like this. But the other night had cracked something open, something raw and dangerous.

His fingers flexed against the wheel before he finally spoke. "Reva... about that night..."

She turned her head slightly, waiting.

He hesitated, choosing his words carefully. "I wanted to apologize—"

She cut him off before he could finish. "It was just a moment, Angad." Her voice was too casual, too light. "We were both feeling vulnerable. It happened. No big deal. Let's not talk about it."

Angad stilled.

No big deal.

His stomach twisted, an unfamiliar weight settling in his chest.

So that was how she saw it.

His jaw clenched, his grip on the steering wheel tightening painfully. In the last week, he had thought about that kiss more times than he cared to admit. The way she had responded to him. The way he had lost himself in her. It had *meant* something. At least to him.

But to her?

She was brushing it off as if it were nothing.

He kept his expression neutral, his voice even. "Right."

And then he said nothing more, just kept driving.

Reva exhaled slowly, staring out the window.

She saw something pass through his eyes—quick and unsettling. But he didn't contradict her. Didn't argue. Didn't say *anything.*

Which only proved what she already knew.

She had been right to stop him.

Because if there was one thing she refused to do ever again, it was fall for a man who didn't want her the same way.

***

CHAPTER EIGHTEEN

THE DINNER

Dinner started off light. Comfortable, even.

Reva and Angad settled into their seats, ordering drinks while the buzz of the restaurant filled the air around them. It wasn't awkward, but it wasn't exactly easy either—there was something about being out with him, just the two of them, that made her hyper-aware of every small thing.

Then, just as their appetizers arrived, Angad's phone buzzed.

Video call from Naina's phone.

The call connected, and in an instant, the twins' excited faces filled the screen, their eyes alight with anticipation.

"Daddy!" Anika shrieked, bouncing on her toes. "Guess what? Our plane is HUGE!"

Avik, standing beside her, waved his boarding pass. "And they gave us these cool stickers!"

Angad chuckled. "Stickers, huh? Let me see."

Avik held the boarding pass up to the camera, making the screen blur for a moment before the small airline logo came into focus. "See? And the air hostess gave me two because I said *please.*"

Anika huffed. "I got two also, but I gave one to Sanaya."

Raj's voice came from the background, amused. "They've been standing here for ten minutes just staring at it as if it's a spaceship."

"Nanu, it's HUGE!" Avik repeated as if the old man hadn't quite grasped the significance of the moment.

Angad raised an eyebrow. "Bigger than the plane we took from New York?"

Avik paused, considering. "Okay… maybe not that big. But still big!"

Anika turned the phone, making the image shake before it steadied, revealing the aircraft parked outside the terminal. "Look, Daddy! That's our plane!"

Angad took in the sight—the sleek white body, the blinking lights. The kids' sheer excitement made him smile, but beneath it, a tug in his chest was evident.

Naina's laughter rang out. "They even tried counting the windows."

"I counted fifty before I got bored," Anika declared proudly.

Reva, watching quietly beside Angad, smirked. "That's because you talk more than you count, little one."

Anika gasped. "Reedi! That's not true!"

Avik elbowed her. "It's a little true."

Raj and Naina appeared behind them, both smiling. "They've already made friends with the air hostess," Raj said, shaking his head.

"Daddy, where are you?" Avik asked suddenly, squinting at the screen.

Angad hesitated. "Uh—"

Before he could answer, Reva leaned in, her voice teasing. "We're having dinner."

"Just the two of you?" Anika asked, eyes widening.

Reva chuckled. "Yes."

Angad sighed, then gave in with a small, amused shake of his head. "Your Reedi has taken me out for dinner."

"What! You both never take us out for dinner," Anika huffed, crossing her arms.

Angad chuckled. "That's because you two are off to Mumbai."

Reva leaned in with a playful smile. "And didn't you make me promise to take care of your daddy?"

The twins exchanged a look before breaking into matching grins.

"Then you HAVE to promise," Avik insisted. "When we come back, we all go out for dinner together!"

Raj smirked in the background, and Naina was barely holding back her grin.

Angad exhaled, a reluctant smile on his lips. "Fine. I promise."

"Pinky promise?" Avik insisted.

He sighed dramatically and held up his pinky. "Pinky promise."

The boarding announcement echoed through the terminal. The twins' faces shifted slightly—still excited, but now mixed with realization.

"Daddy," Avik said, voice softening. "They're calling us."

Angad nodded, gripping the phone a little tighter. "Have fun, okay? And behave."

"We always behave!" Anika protested.

Angad snorted. "That is a blatant lie."

Naina smiled at Angad. "We'll make sure they call as soon as we land. Don't worry."

As the call ended, Angad stared at the blank screen for a moment before letting out a wry chuckle.

"I already miss them," he admitted, more to himself than to her. "And they haven't even boarded yet."

Reva softened. "That just means you're a great dad, Angad."

He looked at her—briefly, intently—something shifting in his eyes. But he didn't reply.

They moved on to dinner.

It was... nice.

The conversation flowed, dipping between casual banter and comfortable silences. Reva let herself relax just a little. They talked about the kids, about food, about work, and about random things that didn't hold much weight, yet felt easy.

At some point, Reva excused herself to go to the washroom. When she returned, she spotted Angad speaking to the waiter, slipping his card onto the tray.

She stopped mid-step.

"Oh, come on!" she groaned as she reached the table. "Angad, I invited you to dinner!"

He didn't so much as glance up. "And I accepted."

"That means you don't get to pay!"

"That's exactly what it means." He punched in his card PIN with an infuriatingly calm expression.

Reva crossed her arms. "You do realize it's okay to let someone else take care of things for once?"

His smirk deepened. "I do. Just not when it comes to feeding you. Now, let's finish the drinks, we both have a long week ahead. The launch is in a few days, and we need to get everything sorted."

She huffed, ready to argue more, when she saw *him* entering the restaurant.

Angad noticed immediately—how she suddenly stiffened, her fingers tightening around her glass, how her entire body seemed to lock up.

Then, just as his brows furrowed in concern, she did something unexpected.

She reached for him.

Without realizing it, her hand landed on Angad's forearm, gripping it a little too tightly.

Angad's eyes flicked down to her hand, then back to her face—she wasn't looking at him. Her gaze was locked on something across the room.

He followed her line of sight.

A man stood near the entrance, dressed in an expensive suit, a smug expression on his face, and a beautiful woman on his arm. The way Reva's nails dug into his skin told Angad everything before she even said a word.

"Who is he?" Angad asked, his voice low, steady.

Reva swallowed, finally tearing her gaze away from the man to glance at Angad. "Someone I used to know."

Before Angad could say anything else, the bastard started walking toward them.

Reva's hand twitched against Angad's arm, but she didn't let go.

Angad went completely still.

The man strode up with an air of easy arrogance, his eyes sweeping over Reva from head to toe, lingering in a way that made Angad's grip on his glass tighten.

"Reva?"

She froze.

Angad didn't miss the way her fingers clenched subtly on his arm, her breath hitching just enough to be noticed. He exhaled slowly, setting his own glass down with deliberate care before reaching to her, covering her hand with his. A quiet, steady weight. A silent reassurance.

The gesture didn't go unnoticed by the man. His gaze flicked to where Angad's hand rested over Reva's, something sharp and fleeting crossing his eyes before his lips curved into a smirk.

"Well, well. Imagine running into you here."

Angad felt Reva stiffen under his touch, and his fingers instinctively pressed a fraction tighter. Steady. Grounding. He didn't speak, didn't move—just watched her.

Reva's throat was dry. She forced a polite smile. "Manish."

Manish relaxed slightly, a smirk playing on his lips. "It's been a long time. You look… good." His gaze dragged over her again, slow and deliberate. Then, without hesitation, Manish leaned in—clearly aiming to kiss Reva on the cheek.

But she turned her face just in time, letting his lips graze only her hair instead.

The misfire caught him off guard. He pulled back quickly, covering the awkward beat with a forced grin, but the flash of irritation in his eyes didn't go unnoticed.

Angad didn't move. He didn't need to. The air around him had shifted. His jaw locked, something sharp and possessive slicing through him.

Manish finally shifted his attention, eyes flicking toward Angad with calculated curiosity. "And aren't you going to introduce me to your... *friend*?"

Reva's voice came out a little too fast, a little too forced. "Oh, he's Angad Sareen. Angad, this is Manish Suri."

Manish's eyes gleamed with recognition, and he extended a hand with exaggerated enthusiasm. "Of course! Angad Sareen. Who doesn't know you? Your reputation precedes you."

Angad didn't take the offered handshake.

He just stared. Cold. Unmoving.

Manish let out a low chuckle, dropping his hand. "I've read about you. Big name in the media world. In fact, I've been meaning to get in touch with you for a business proposal."

Angad didn't respond. Didn't blink. Just took a slow sip of his drink, gaze unwavering, unreadable.

Manish's smirk didn't falter. His gaze flicked back to Reva, amusement dancing in his eyes. "So, how do you two know each other?"

None of your damn business, Angad nearly said.

"Work," Reva answered curtly, her tone leaving no room for further questions.

Angad's fingers curled around his glass. *Work? That's all it was?*

"You're working with him now?" Manish said, a hint of mock admiration in his tone. "That's impressive."

Angad didn't like his tone.

Didn't like the way Manish was looking at Reva.

Didn't like any of this.

His fingers flexed against the table, resisting the urge to pull Reva closer to remind this bastard exactly who he was dealing with. Instead, he finally spoke, his voice cool, measured.

"Pleasure." *It wasn't.*

Manish grinned, oblivious—or maybe just enjoying himself too much. "Well, don't let me interrupt your evening. Reva, we should catch up sometime."

Angad had heard enough.

"You already have," he said, his tone cool.

Manish blinked. "Sorry?"

"The evening," Angad clarified. "You've already interrupted it. Goodbye."

Manish blinked, clearly caught off guard by the blunt dismissal. But then he smirked again, giving Reva one last lingering look before walking away.

Reva let out a slow breath she hadn't realized she was holding, her grip on Angad loosening.

Angad didn't speak. He simply reached for his glass, took a slow sip, and watched her.

She refused to look at him. Instead, she grabbed her purse. "Ready to go?"

He didn't push. Didn't ask.

Not yet.

*

The drive home was quiet. Not the comfortable kind—the one charged with tension, with words unsaid and thoughts unspoken.

Angad kept his eyes on the road, but every few moments, he glanced at her. Reva sat stiffly, arms crossed over her stomach, staring out the window, lost in a world he wasn't part of. Whatever memories Manish had stirred up, they still had their claws in her.

By the time they pulled up to her building, she reached for the door handle almost on autopilot. But before she could step out, Angad hesitated.

"Wanna talk?"

She stilled. Fingers curled around the handle, her body half-turned toward him.

Then she exhaled, shaking her head. "Too long a story."

Angad leaned back against his seat. "I have nowhere to be."

That made her pause. Her grip loosened. For a long moment, she simply looked at him, something shifting across her face—uncertain, unspoken. Then, slowly, she nodded.

Angad parked the car. Without a word, he stepped out and followed her inside.

Once they reached her apartment, she tossed her purse onto the entryway table and exhaled. "Wine or coffee?"

He didn't even have to think about it. "Whatever you need right now."

Her lips curved—tired but appreciative. "Wine it is."

A few minutes later, they were out on the balcony again. The garden and the pool were illuminated below. The air was cool but not cold. The same spot as the other evening. Only this time, the silence between them wasn't loaded with the weight of their kiss. It was heavier.

Reva took a sip of her drink and set it down. Then, without looking at him, she spoke.

"Ask," she repeated his words.

He turned to her. "What did he do to you?"

Reva drew in a slow, measured breath—the kind that steadied, that braced.

"He dated me," she said quietly. "Not for me. For what I could give him."

Angad didn't respond, just watched her, waiting.

She traced the rim of her glass, eyes distant. "We got engaged after just a few weeks of knowing each other. I was naïve. In love. Manish was charming, ambitious—a guy trying to carve a place for himself in the business world. He came from new money, and he never let anyone forget it. And I..." she exhaled a humorless laugh. "I wanted to believe he loved me."

Angad's grip tightened around his glass, his jaw ticking, but he said nothing.

"But... he didn't. Not really." She kept her glass in hand, knuckles whitening slightly, though she made no move to drink. "He loved what I could do for him. The doors I could open, the people I knew. My family's connections," her fingers tightened around the glass. "And when he didn't need them anymore, he didn't need me either."

She lifted her chin, forcing a small, brittle smile. "So, he cheated. And then dumped me."

Angad exhaled slowly, watching her.

She mirrored his breath, eyes fixed on the deep burgundy hue in her glass. It caught the light, but her gaze wasn't on the drink—it was somewhere far away, locked in memories that still lingered. When she finally spoke, her voice was calm, almost too calm. Like it had practiced being steady.

"It was my birthday," she said. "The one night that was supposed to be about me. I'd been excited, hoping maybe—just maybe—he had planned something special. A surprise. Something meaningful." A humorless laugh escaped her. "And in a way, it was a surprise."

Angad remained silent, watching her.

"I walked into his apartment," she continued, her voice steady but tight, fingers clenched around the glass. "And there they were—so completely absorbed in each other, so certain in their betrayal… it was like I had never been part of his world at all."

Angad's grip on his own drink turned white-knuckled.

"She was younger. Effortlessly beautiful," Reva said, her mouth curving into something between a smile and a grimace. "And he—" she drew in a breath, steadying herself. "He didn't even flinch. No guilt. Just… annoyance, like I'd interrupted something trivial."

Angad's jaw ticked, his expression neutral. But his fingers flexed on the armrest as if resisting the urge to reach for her.

"It was not because he fell out of love," she continued, her voice steady but soft. "But because he was never in love in the first place."

Silence.

She turned to him then, looking at him as if daring him to react. To judge. To pity.

But all he did was pick up his glass, take a sip, and say, "What an idiot!"

Reva blinked. This was not the reaction she expected.

Angad shrugged, leaning back. "He had *you*, and he threw it away… for what? Business connections? Money? Another woman?" He scoffed, shaking his head. "Idiot."

Something in her face shifted. The tension in her shoulders loosened just a little.

A small, real smile touched her lips. "Yeah," she murmured. "He was."

She lifted her glass in a mock toast.

As their glasses met with a quiet clink, their eyes held—just for a beat too long. A silent echo of something unspoken, something lingering between them. The memory of a kiss that had burned too bright to forget.

Reva's fingers tightened around her glass, her breath hitching ever so slightly. Angad's gaze dipped—just a fraction—to her lips. And for a fleeting second, the air between them thickened, heavy with the pull of something neither of them had the courage to name.

Then his phone buzzed again, shattering the moment.

A video call. The kids.

Angad exhaled, setting his glass down before answering. "Hey, guys."

Anika's excited face filled the screen, her curls bouncing as she shifted. "Daddy, we landed! Nanu says we'll be at Sanaya's home soon—wait…"

Suddenly, Sanaya leaned in, her brows scrunching as she peered at the background. "Are you at Maasi's house, Angad Uncle?"

Silence. A charged, awkward silence.

Avik's curious face popped up next, eyes squinting as if trying to confirm Sanaya's observation.

Angad hesitated, glancing at Reva, who blinked at him, equally taken aback.

Then, with practiced ease, he leaned back and subtly adjusted the camera angle. "Just winding down for the evening, Avik," he said smoothly, offering nothing more.

Avik's gaze sharpened with all the suspicion of a five-year-old who missed nothing. "But that looks like Reedi's house."

Reva cleared her throat, stepping in. "Hey, guys! How was the flight? Didn't you just land? You must be tired."

"Not really." Anika grinned. "But, Reedi, why is Daddy at your house? Are you having a sleepover?"

Reva nearly choked on her wine.

Angad coughed, reaching for his own drink like it might help. "Anika, did you get your bags yet?"

Naina's voice floated in from the background, clearly amused. "She got them. Don't worry about the kids. You both enjoy your evening. We'll call in the morning. The kids are exhausted."

"We're not!" Three voices protested in unison.

Reva bit back a laugh, hiding it behind her glass.

Angad shook his head, his lips twitching despite himself. "Alright, kids, listen to Nanu-Nani. Go home, get some sleep. We'll talk tomorrow."

Anika pouted but waved. "Okay. Bye, Daddy. Bye, Reedi."

The call ended, leaving them in silence once more.

Angad stared at the blank screen for a second before putting his phone in his pocket. He hesitated, then exhaled. "I should get going."

Reva nodded, though something inside her twisted, sinking low.

She didn't stop him.

And just like that, he was gone.

***

CHAPTER NINTEEN

THE BREAKING POINT

The days leading up to the website launch blurred into a whirlwind of work and long hours, each moment charged with an undercurrent of something neither of them acknowledged but both undeniably felt.

Reva and Angad spent more time together than they ever had before. Mornings began with Angad picking Reva up; their drives were filled with quiet conversations, lingering glances, and occasional brushes of fingers.

Evenings stretched late into the night, dinners at their desks turning into dinners outside the office. He always dropped her home. Always waited until she was inside. But he never came up.

Still, the space between them was shrinking.

At work, their eyes found each other across the conference room table. A fleeting look. A knowing glance. Small, accidental touches—a brush of hands as they reached for the same document, a press of his palm against the small of her back as he guided her through a crowded hallway—each one leaving an imprint far deeper than it should have.

And then there were the calls. Every day, without fail, the kids would call as promised. It had become routine. If Reva and Angad were together, they would greet her with the same excitement as they did their father. But on the rare occasion she wasn't there, they noticed.

"Where's Reedi?" Anika had asked just last evening, her curious little face peeking into the screen as he was about to leave the office.

Angad sighed, running a hand over his face. "She must be at her place. Where else?"

"But she's always with you," Avik pointed out, tilting his head as if trying to solve a puzzle.

Sanaya jumped in then, her grin mischievous. "Maybe she finally got tired of your grumpy face, Angad Uncle."

Reva, who had been sitting on the other side of the couch, listening in, had barely managed to stifle her laughter.

The calls only added to the tension that was already brewing between them. The familiarity. The comfort. It was beginning to feel like she belonged in parts of his life he had never intended to let anyone into.

And yet, the tension built.

It was there in the way Angad would linger outside her building some nights, fingers tapping against the steering wheel, something unsaid hanging in the air before he finally murmured a good night. It was in the way Reva hesitated at her doorstep, knowing she should go inside but inexplicably wanting to stay just a little longer.

Something was bound to give. They just didn't know when.

Or how.

And now, it was already Friday night—the launch event.

The venue was a high-end party lounge, the kind that exuded understated elegance, much like Angad himself. The press, industry leaders, and the entire editorial and tech teams were in attendance, all eager to witness Angad's latest venture.

Angad had been mid-conversation with a potential investor when he saw her. The words stopped forming. The man's voice across from him blurred into background static, and all he could focus on—was her.

Reva.

She had told him she'd get to the venue on her own—and now, here she was.

She moved like she didn't need anyone's permission to exist in that space. Her gown—black, sculpted, devastating—fit her like it had been crafted to trace every inch of her strength and softness. The asymmetrical neckline exposed the slope of her shoulder, skin glowing under the crystal lights. The draped folds at her waist shifted just enough with her stride to remind him of how she moved when she wasn't trying to be seen.

Angad felt something tighten in his chest.

He had seen her in simple kurtas and jeans, hair tied up as she argued over headlines, in crisp office wear that matched her no-nonsense tone during meetings, in anger and laughter and silence. But he had never seen her like this—graceful, still, and quietly stunning in a way that stole the air from his lungs.

He adjusted his collar, cleared his throat. Said something vague to the man beside him. But his gaze didn't leave her.

He couldn't.

The evening unfolded smoothly. Speeches, presentations, and a showcase of the new website's features. Reva was by his side through it all—fine-tuning last-minute details, handling the press, and making sure everything ran seamlessly.

Now, the night was winding down. The drinks flowed, the congratulations poured in, and the tension between them crackled just beneath the surface.

Reva stood near the bar, sipping on a glass of wine, finally taking a moment to breathe. Across the room, Angad was in conversation with a group of investors, but his eyes flicked toward her every few minutes. She felt it—his gaze, the weight of it, the way it skimmed over her bare shoulder, down the fitted dress she had chosen without really thinking about what it would do to him.

He wasn't the only one watching her.

Rohit Arora, a smooth talker from a rival media company, had lingered at her side far too long. He laughed at something she said, leaning in, his hand grazing her arm in a way that made her stiffen. She was just about to step away when a voice, firm and unmistakable, cut through the conversation.

"Reva."

She turned, finding Angad standing there, gaze dark, expression stern.

Rohit straightened, offering a polite smile. "Ah, Mr. Sareen. Incredible launch tonight. You've got a powerhouse on your team here." He nodded toward Reva, eyes glinting with something that made her stomach turn.

Angad's jaw ticked. "I know." His voice was measured, but his grip on the glass in his hand was anything but.

Reva exhaled, willing the sudden tension to ease.

Rohit turned back to her. "You're a freelance consultant, right?"

She nodded. "Yes."

His smile widened. "Good. I'd also like to consult with you. I'll fix up a meeting soon."

Angad stilled.

Reva felt the shift—the way his posture turned rigid, the slight flex of his fingers around his glass, like a man barely restraining himself.

She kept her expression smooth, professional. "Of course. Let me know when it works for you."

"Excellent." Rohit glanced at Angad, his smile lingering, before lifting his drink. "I'll be in touch."

As he walked away, Reva turned back to Angad, whose jaw was still clenched tight.

She placed a hand on his forearm, her voice light and careful. "I was just heading home," she said smoothly, hoping to diffuse the moment.

But Angad didn't move. Didn't speak.

Not until his gaze finally dropped to her—dark, steady, impossible to read.

"I'll take you," he said.

She blinked, thrown off by the quiet authority in his tone. A shiver curled down her spine.

Because there was something in his tone, something different.

And she wasn't sure either of them could stop what was coming next.

Her eyes wavered. "Okay."

*

The car ride was thick with unspoken words. Reva stole a glance at Angad, his profile illuminated by the city lights flashing past the windows. His fingers drummed against the steering wheel, his jaw locked tight.

She sighed. "Are you going to tell me what that was back there?"

His grip tightened. "What?"

She huffed a quiet laugh, shaking her head. "You know what."

Silence. Then—

"You let men like that get too close," he muttered.

Her brows shot up. "Men like *that*?"

"Men who think they can have you." His voice was lower now, rougher. "Men who don't even know what they'd be getting."

Her breath hitched. "And you do?"

His jaw tightened. Did he?

He knew what it was like to want her. Knew what it was like to crave the fire in her eyes, the sharp wit on her tongue, the softness she kept so carefully guarded. He knew she wasn't just a beautiful woman in a room full of men who thought they could have her. She was more. More than they could ever understand. More than he had any right to want.

And yet, he did.

But he couldn't say that. Not when he was barely holding himself back. Not when he had no right to stake a claim, he wasn't sure he could keep.

So, instead, he let the silence stretch.

As they neared her building, Angad exhaled sharply, shaking his head as if trying to clear it. The tension between them had been building for days, pressing down on them like a storm waiting to break. He pulled into her building's driveway, but instead of putting the car in park, he hesitated.

He turned to her then, the weight of his gaze making her pulse skitter. "Come with me."

Reva's lips parted. "What?"

"I don't want to drop you off." His voice was quiet, but there was something raw beneath it. Something that made her stomach tighten. "Not tonight."

She should say no. She should laugh it off, step out of the car, and pretend none of this was happening.

But she didn't. She nodded.

***

CHAPTER TWENTY

NO GOING BACK

His place was silent when they entered. The staff had left for the evening. The house felt too still, too charged with everything unsaid between them. Reva walked in slowly, taking in the space she had only ever seen once. It had felt like him—warm, controlled, with hints of a life he didn't often let people see.

The familiarity of it settled over her, but it felt different now. Then, she had sat in his living room, shared a meal with him and his children, glimpsed a version of him that was softer, quieter. A father. A man who, despite everything, put his kids first.

But tonight, it was just the two of them.

The room felt smaller. The air heavier.

It *still* felt like him—warm, controlled, with hints of a life he didn't often let people see.

But now, she was seeing more of it. More of him.

More than she had any business wanting.

She turned, only to find him watching her, the air between them thick, almost suffocating. "Why didn't you drop me home?"

Angad met her gaze, his own unreadable. "You know why."

She tilted her head, waiting. "Say it."

His jaw clenched, the war inside him evident—the same battle he'd been fighting for days. Weeks. Maybe longer.

"I didn't want to." The words came rough, dragged from deep within.

Her breath hitched, but she held his gaze. "Why did you bring me here?"

His restraint was slipping, crumbling under the weight of everything he wanted but knew he shouldn't have. His fingers flexed at his sides before he finally exhaled, defeated.

The moment hung between them, thick with tension, unspoken words crackling in the air. Angad took a step closer, his body taut, his gaze locked onto hers as if daring her to stop him. But she didn't. She wouldn't.

His fingers brushed against her arm, trailing up to her shoulder, his touch slow, deliberate, giving her every opportunity to pull away. Reva stood still, heart hammering against her ribs, anticipation thrumming through her veins. When his palm finally cupped her cheek, she leaned into it, eyes half-lidded, lips parting just slightly.

"Because I couldn't let you go. Not tonight," he murmured again, his thumb tracing the curve of her jaw.

"Then don't," she whispered back.

That was all it took. His restraint shattered.

The first touch wasn't hesitant—it was desperate, urgent. His hands found her waist, pulling her against him as his lips claimed hers, firm and demanding, his body pressing her back against the wall. The kiss was nothing like the one from days ago—it was hotter, hungrier, a raw collision of need and desire. She gasped against his mouth, and he seized the opportunity, deepening the kiss, his tongue stroking against hers, coaxing, teasing.

Her fingers gripped his shirt, anchoring herself as heat coiled low in her belly. His hands skimmed down her sides, mapping the curves he had long tried to ignore. When he gripped her waist, pulling her flush against him, she felt the full extent of his desire, and it sent a shudder through her.

When he lifted her effortlessly, her legs wrapped around his waist, and she felt herself being carried, guided through the dimly lit house until her back met the cool wood of his bedroom door.

His lips left hers for a moment, just long enough for his gaze to search hers for one final moment of clarity.

She whispered, "Don't stop."

And he didn't.

They barely made it into his bedroom. Angad's lips never left hers, his hands never stopped roaming. By the time he backed her against the bed, her skin was on fire. He pulled away just enough to search her face, his breathing ragged.

"Reva…" His voice was hoarse, laced with restraint. "Are you sure?"

She met his gaze, unwavering. "Yes."

But when he reached for the zipper of her dress, his fingers slowing with reverence, something flickered in her expression—a hesitation, not of doubt but of unfamiliarity. His brows furrowed as a sliver of doubt struck him.

His body tensed. His breath hitched. His hands stilled against her.

For a moment, he simply looked at her, his gaze searching, questioning. Not for permission—he already had that—but for understanding.

Reva swallowed, suddenly aware of the way his fingers rested against her spine, of how the air between them thickened, pulsing with anticipation. She had never been undressed like this before. Not with this kind of intent. Not with a man who made her feel like she might shatter from just a look.

Angad's eyes darkened, his jaw tightening as if he sensed her hesitation. "Reva..." His voice was low, steady, patient. He dragged his knuckles down her arm, a featherlight touch that sent shivers through her. "Tell me if you need me to stop."

She shook her head, exhaling slowly. "I don't."

That was all he needed.

He slid the zipper down, his knuckles grazing her spine as he peeled the dress from her shoulder. The fabric loosened, slipping down her body and pooling at her feet in a quiet whisper.

His breath faltered.

Reva resisted the urge to cover herself, to fold her arms over her stomach, to hide. Years of self-doubt—of knowing she didn't have the kind of body that effortlessly turned heads—clawed at her. She had curves, soft lines where others were lean. She wasn't small or delicate, not one of those women who exuded picture-perfect charm without trying.

And yet, Angad looked at her like she was something to be worshipped.

His fingers traced down her arms, slow, reverent. "You're beautiful."

She let out a shaky breath. "You don't have to say that."

His gaze snapped to hers, sharp and unyielding. "I don't say anything I don't mean."

Then he touched her.

His hands framed her waist, his thumbs stroking her bare skin. He bent, his lips brushing over her shoulder, then lower, following the curve of her body as if memorizing every inch. His mouth burned a path along her skin, a silent devotion, a vow.

Reva's pulse pounded as he reached behind her, unhooking her bra with a practiced ease. He gave her time, waiting for her to push him away, to hesitate. But she didn't.

When the lace slipped down from her, she held her breath.

Angad exhaled sharply, his fingers tightening on her waist. "Fuck." The raw hunger in his voice made her toes curl.

His eyes roved over her, dark and smoldering, taking in the swell of her breasts, the smooth curve of her stomach, the soft vulnerability of her.

And then he kissed her again—harder, deeper. Not just with need but with something that felt dangerously close to worship.

She shivered as his hands trailed lower, over the band of her underwear, dragging them down with aching slowness. When she was bare before him, his gaze darkened further, his nostrils flaring as if he was holding himself back.

Reva felt exposed. Seen in a way she never had been before.

But not once did he look at her with anything less than raw, unfiltered desire.

She swallowed hard, her hands trembling as she reached for his shirt. He let her unbutton it, her fingers brushing over hard planes and taut muscles. When she pushed it off his shoulders, she finally saw him—the broad chest, the sculpted lines, the faint dusting of hair leading down...

Her throat went dry.

He was... beautiful. Strong, carved, every inch of him honed.

Angad watched her reaction.

"You're staring," he murmured, his lips ghosting over her ear.

Her cheeks burned. "So are you."

His hands slid up her arms, back to her face, tilting it upward. "That's because I can't help myself."

He caught her mouth again, deep and slow, pulling her against him—bare skin to bare skin.

And in that moment, her insecurities melted away.

Here, like this, she wasn't just a woman who had spent years hiding behind her own doubts.

She was his.

And she didn't want to hold back anymore.

Reva's fingers trembled as they moved to his belt. She had never done this before—never undressed a man like this, never taken the lead when every fiber of her body burned with anticipation.

Angad stood still, watching her with an intensity that sent shivers down her spine. He was letting her set the pace, waiting for her to decide.

Her breath hitched as she unfastened the buckle, her fingers grazing the hard plane of his stomach. She tugged the leather free, then moved to the button of his trousers. It popped open easily, the zipper following with a soft rasp that somehow made her pulse throb harder.

She hesitated, her fingers curling around the waistband.

His voice was low, rough. "Reva."

She looked up, meeting his eyes—dark, smoldering, filled with a hunger he wasn't bothering to hide.

"You don't have to be nervous," he murmured, his thumb brushing over her cheek, a stark contrast to the way his body radiated tension. "But if you keep looking at me like that, I might lose my patience."

Something in his tone sent a thrill down her spine.

Reva exhaled and pushed his trousers down, letting them pool at his feet. He stepped out of them, his movements slow and deliberate. Her gaze shifted lower, to the final barrier between them—black boxer briefs that did nothing to hide just how much he wanted her.

Her mouth went dry.

She had imagined this moment before—wondered what he looked like beneath his perfectly tailored suits, beneath the crisp dress shirts that only hinted at the body beneath.

But nothing had prepared her for this.

He was all hard muscle and raw masculinity, with broad shoulders tapering to a lean waist; every inch of him was honed and powerful.

And then he reached for her hand, guiding it to the waistband of his briefs.

Her pulse thundered. She curled her fingers around the fabric, hesitating for only a second before she dragged them down.

The moment he was bare before her, a sharp gasp left her lips.

God.

He was… big. Thick, hard, every inch of him aroused and aching.

Heat pooled in her stomach as she swallowed hard, her eyes widening just slightly. She had never seen a man like this before—not in real life, not this close, not in a way that felt so utterly… overwhelming.

Angad's lips twitched, his voice laced with amusement. "Reva."

Her gaze snapped up to meet his, and she realized he was watching her reaction closely, triumph glinting in his eyes.

"I..." She exhaled shakily, unable to find the words.

He slid his hand around her waist, gentle but possessive. "You're killing me, sweetheart."

Her breath hitched at the endearment, at the raw need in his voice.

And then he kissed her again, deep and desperate, pressing her back until her bare body molded against his.

The sensation was electric. Skin against skin, heat against heat.

All thoughts vanished as his hands gripped her hips, his mouth trailing fire down her neck, lower, lower...

And when he lifted her effortlessly, carrying her toward the bed, she knew—she would never be the same after this night.

Because this wasn't just passion.

This was Angad.

And there was no coming back from him.

Angad laid her down with a gentleness that contradicted the raw hunger in his eyes. His body covered hers, the heat of his skin branding her, making her shiver despite the fire raging inside her.

His mouth traced a slow, reverent path from her collarbone to the swell of her breasts, his hands mapping every curve, every dip of her body. His touch made her feel worshipped, cherished—like she was something rare, something he couldn't get enough of.

Reva's breath hitched as his lips closed around one aching peak, his tongue flicking over her sensitive flesh. A gasp escaped her, her fingers diving into his hair, nails grazing his scalp as she arched into him, silently begging for more.

He gave her more.

His hands skimmed down her sides, over the softness she had always been self-conscious about. But there was no hesitation, no restraint in the way he touched her. If anything, he seemed to savor every inch of her, murmuring low, filthy praises against her skin that sent molten heat pooling between her thighs.

When his fingers found her core, sliding through her slick folds, she jolted, a whimper spilling from her lips.

"You're so ready for me," he rasped, his forehead resting against hers, his breath uneven. "I need you to tell me if—"

"Yes," she gasped, already trembling. "Angad, please."

A curse slipped past his lips. He shifted, positioning himself between her thighs, his hands bracketing her hips as he lined himself up.

Then, slowly, he pushed inside.

The stretch was more than she had anticipated, an unfamiliar pressure that made her body tense for a second—until he stilled, his breathing ragged, his control hanging by a thread.

His forehead dropped to hers, his jaw clenched. "Fuck, Reva… you're so—" He exhaled sharply, his doubt confirmed. His fingers flexed on her waist as if grounding himself. "Are you okay?"

She nodded, her breath shallow, adjusting to the fullness of him. "Yes."

"Tell me if—"

"Don't stop." Her nails bit into his shoulders, her thighs tightening around his hips. "Please."

That single word undid him.

Angad groaned, his restraint snapping. He pulled back slightly before thrusting in again, deeper this time, his movements slow, deliberate, as if he wanted her to feel everything.

And she did.

Every inch of him.

Every stroke that had her body arching, every whispered curse against her skin, every desperate sound she couldn't hold back.

She clung to him, lost in the rhythm he set, lost in the way he made her feel—like she was the only thing that mattered, like he had been waiting for this just as long as she had.

Their bodies moved in perfect sync, the tension coiling tighter and tighter until she shattered, pleasure crashing over her in waves so intense, she cried out his name, her nails dragging down his back.

Angad followed with a strangled groan, his body tensing before he gave in, his release spilling into her as he buried his face in the crook of her neck.

For a long moment, neither of them moved. Their breaths mingled, bodies still entwined, hearts pounding in sync.

And then, slowly, he lifted his head, brushing damp strands of hair from her face.

"You okay?" he murmured, his voice hoarse, his thumb stroking her cheek.

Reva let out a breathless laugh, still floating, still trying to process what had just happened.

"More than okay."

A slow, wicked smirk tugged at his lips. "Good."

He kissed her again.

It wasn't just desperation or need. It was something more. Something that rooted itself deep inside him, something he wasn't ready to name.

But he knew this—there was no going back.

***

CHAPTER TWENTY ONE

THE CALM BEFORE

The Saturday morning sun streamed through the curtains, painting golden patterns across the tangled sheets. The room was steeped in the quiet aftermath of the night before, the air still carrying the warmth of shared whispers, of slow-burning desire that had finally, finally been unleashed.

Reva stirred, warmth curling through her as she felt the solid weight of Angad's arm draped possessively over her waist. His fingers moved in slow, idle strokes over the curve of her hip, tracing lazy patterns against her bare skin as if committing every inch of her to memory.

She exhaled softly, her body still deliciously sore, a reminder of how thoroughly he had claimed her.

"Morning," his voice was husky, rough with sleep, lips grazing her bare shoulder, the warmth of his breath sending a shiver down her spine.

She stretched against him, arching slightly, a small hum escaping her lips as the movement made her acutely aware of just how intimately tangled they still were. "Morning."

He shifted, propping himself on one elbow, his gaze sweeping over her face as if seeing her in this light—bare, vulnerable, in his bed—was something he hadn't allowed himself to truly believe until now.

His fingers brushed a stray strand of hair from her cheek, lingering as he cupped her face. "How does it feel?"

She blinked up at him, her heart giving a slow, traitorous thud. "You mean after last night?"

A corner of his mouth lifted, but his eyes remained serious, searching. "Yeah."

She met his gaze, her voice quiet but sure. "I'm okay."

She studied him, the tension in his shoulders, the way his thumb ghosted over her cheekbone as if afraid she'd disappear. Something about the way he asked made her chest tighten—not because she had doubts, but because he cared enough to.

Instead of answering right away, she let her fingers explore—the steady rise and fall of his chest, the morning stubble shadowing his sharp jaw, the heat of his skin under her touch. She traced his collarbone, following the sculpted lines of him, the body that had held her, worshiped her, made her feel beautiful in a way she hadn't allowed herself to in a long time.

Then, his voice dipped, laced with the slightest trace of doubt, "Did I hurt you?"

She saw the concern in his gaze, the way his fingers paused against her skin as if bracing for an answer he didn't want to hear.

She bit her lip, then gently took his hand and placed it over her chest, letting him feel the steady rhythm of her heartbeat beneath his palm. "A little," she admitted honestly, watching his jaw clench, his brows pull together. Before he could say anything, she traced his lower lip with her thumb, a small, reassuring smile playing on hers. "But it was worth it."

His breath left him in a slow exhale, tension melting from his shoulders. He held her tighter, his grip firm but careful, like he wanted to both shield and worship her at the same time.

His hand slid lower, tracing the line of her waist, his fingers skimming over the dip of her spine. "It was," he murmured, voice rough.

His eyes then searched hers, holding her there, grounding her. "Why now?"

The question sent a shiver through her—not because she didn't know the answer, but because saying it aloud made it real.

She hesitated, fingers stilling over his chest. "Because it felt right."

His expression didn't change, but something in his eyes darkened, his grip on her tightening ever so slightly. As if her words carried more weight than she even realized.

She swallowed, her heart hammering as he shifted closer, pressing her back into the pillows. He was warm, solid, his body fitting against hers like he had always belonged there.

He kissed her then—not urgent, not demanding, but slow and deep, a kiss that tasted of morning heat and unspoken promises.

And when he moved over her again, his name left her lips in a sigh, her body arching instinctively to meet him.

This time, it wasn't about unleashing something long restrained.

It was about something softer, something that wrapped around her and held her close.

And she never wanted to let go.

*

Neither of them registered the silent buzz of their phones on the nightstand.

Wrapped in each other, lost in slow kisses and languid touches, the outside world didn't exist. Not the day waiting for them, not the responsibilities looming just beyond the bedroom door.

It wasn't until much later—when their breaths were still uneven, their bodies still tangled in the sheets—that reality began to creep in.

Reva stirred, stretching lazily, a satisfied hum slipping past her lips. But when her gaze flicked toward the bedside clock, her contentment faltered. Her eyes widened.

"Oh my God… look at the time! We slept in so late."

Angad groaned, refusing to open his eyes, his arm tightening around her waist as he pressed a slow, lingering kiss to her bare shoulder. "Worth it."

She huffed a laugh, fingers threading through his disheveled hair. "You're insatiable."

He cracked one eye open, a smirk tugging at the corner of his lips. "Have you seen you?"

Heat crept up her skin at the way he looked at her—like he was still memorizing every inch of her, like he wasn't done worshipping her yet.

Her heart did something traitorous in her chest.

But before she could say anything, he rolled onto his back with a sigh, scrubbing a hand over his face. "Come on, let's get some food in you before I forget how to be a gentleman, and your stomach starts making those angry sounds."

She laughed, shaking her head as she reached for the sheets, wrapping them snugly around her body before sliding off the bed. "Pretty sure you forgot to be a gentleman last night."

Angad stretched lazily, arms behind his head, a smug smirk playing on his lips. "Not forgetting. Prioritizing."

She narrowed her eyes at him but grinned, cheeks warm. "Oh God…" she gasped suddenly, eyes widening.

He sat up, alert. "What?"

"What about Raju?" she whispered, mortified. "What will he think—me walking out of your room like this?"

Angad chuckled, completely unbothered. "I gave him the day off."

She blinked. "When?"

"This morning. Left him a message." He gave a slight shrug like it was the most obvious thing in the world.

A quiet breath of relief escaped her. "Hmm… good. Thank you." She padded over and leaned in to kiss his cheek, her sheet shifting slightly as she moved.

Angad got out of bed, grabbed his boxers from the floor, and slipped them on. As he stood, the morning sun caught the hard lines of his body, the deep grooves of muscle that flexed and moved as he stretched again. Reva's eyes lingered—appreciative, admiring. Her gaze swept over him slowly, heat curling low in her belly.

"Umm… Angad?" she said, breaking the silence, voice softer.

"Yeah?" he looked over his shoulder at her.

She held the sheet tighter, suddenly shy. "Could you… Maybe lend me something to wear?"

He paused mid-step, then turned, one brow arched in mock seriousness. "I mean… I *prefer* the way you are right now."

Her mouth parted in protest, but he wasn't finished.

"Why bother wearing something," he added, his voice dropping suggestively as he closed the gap between them, "when I'm just going to tear it off again after feeding you?"

Reva's jaw dropped, her face coloring instantly. "You're incorrigible," she muttered, eyes wide.

He grinned wickedly, clearly enjoying her flustered reaction. "You're adorable when you blush, you know that?"

She swatted him with a pillow, but he dodged easily, laughing. With a little shake of his head, he walked over to his closet and pulled out a soft grey tee and a pair of drawstring shorts. Handing them to her, his fingers brushed hers deliberately, eyes holding hers for a beat longer than necessary.

"Here. For now," he said, voice low and teasing.

She snatched the clothes, muttering something about needing privacy, and he smirked again, already walking toward the kitchen. "I'll make us coffee," he called over his shoulder. "You get dressed."

*

By the time Reva padded into the kitchen, barefoot and freshly changed, the scent of coffee and toast had already begun to fill the air. Angad stood by the counter, bare-chested, flipping eggs in a pan like it was second nature.

She paused in the doorway, watching him for a moment. The morning light slanted through the blinds, casting golden stripes across his skin. His hair was still deliciously messy, and the soft cotton of his boxers hung low on his hips.

"You cook too?" she asked, amused.

He glanced back with a smirk. "Basic survival skills. Besides, I'm trying to impress the woman who let me ravish her all night."

She laughed, walking over and leaning against the island. "Ravish, huh? That's one word for it."

He looked her up and down slowly, eyes lingering on his oversized tee hanging off her frame. "Looks better on you."

She rolled her eyes, trying not to smile, as she grabbed two mugs from the open shelf. "You really don't have an off switch, do you?"

"Not when you're around." He poured the coffee and slid her a mug. "Milk, no sugar, right?"

She paused, brow raised. "You remembered?"

"I remember everything about you," he said casually, but his tone held something deeper. He turned back to the stove before she could respond.

They ate perched on stools, side by side, knees brushing under the counter. The kind of breakfast that felt like it belonged in a different life—simple, unhurried, comfortable.

Between bites and sips of coffee, they exchanged stories—childhood quirks, work disasters, favorite shows. She teased him for his serious taste in news and politics; he mocked her for crying over fictional characters in books. It was easy, even with the weight of what had happened between them lingering in the air.

At one point, her hand drifted to his arm, fingers tracing the faint scar near his elbow.

"How did you get this?"

"Fell off my bike when I was sixteen. Tried to impress a girl," he said with mock pride.

"Did it work?"

"Nope. She laughed and walked off with my best friend."

Reva giggled. "Serves you right."

He grinned at the sound of her laughter, leaning in to press a kiss to her temple.

As the last sip of coffee disappeared from her mug, Reva stretched again, her fingers brushing the hem of Angad's T-shirt on her thighs. The air between them was still warm with affection, but the clock on the wall didn't lie.

"I should head back," she said softly, eyes dropping to the time. "I have a few things to finish. Dinner tonight?"

Angad stood, stretching his arms above his head with a low groan that made her cheeks flush again. "Let's make it a real date. What time should I pick you up?"

She smiled as she rinsed her mug. "Seven-ish? I'll wear something nice."

He leaned against the counter, arms folded, watching her. "You look perfect right now."

"I'm wearing your clothes," she said.

He shrugged, grinning. "Exactly."

She rolled her eyes and turned to him, brushing imaginary crumbs off his shoulder. "Dinner. Tonight. My treat."

"We'll see," he said, smirking as he leaned in and kissed her forehead.

"Umm… can I leave my dress here?" Reva asked, glancing toward the bedroom with a sheepish smile. "I'll pick it up later."

He nodded, then took a step away. "Let me drop you."

Reva quickly shook her head, hugging her evening clutch closer to her chest. "No, it's fine. It's just a five-minute walk."

He raised an eyebrow. "Still—give me a minute to throw on a shirt, I'll come with you."

She gave him a warm, yet firm, look. "Don't. You've already done enough damage to my composure for one morning."

He chuckled. "At least let me walk you to the elevator?"

Reva shook her head. "Absolutely not. I'm already doing the walk of shame in broad daylight—don't make it worse."

"And you'd still look better than all of Delhi," he muttered.

She shot him a look but couldn't help the laugh that escaped. "I'm walking out of your apartment at twelve-thirty in the afternoon… wearing your clothes. I already feel like a headline."

He leaned against the kitchen wall, grinning. "Better a headline than a footnote."

"Stop being charming," she said over her shoulder.

"And yet, here you are. Already planning dinner," he teased. Then, a beat later, more seriously, "You think anyone will say anything?"

"I *know* they'll talk," she said, exasperated. "Ateliers' gossip network is faster than the internet. Half of them probably are already gossiping about us, with you picking and dropping me every day."

He laughed, backing away with his hands raised in mock surrender. "Alright, alright. No chauffeur treatment. I get it."

Reva gave him a wry smile as she walked to the door. "I need at least five minutes of fresh air to pretend I have some dignity left."

"You have plenty of dignity," he said, still grinning. "But if you're trying to look less ravished, maybe smooth your hair a bit."

She glared at him over her shoulder, cheeks flushing. "You are *not* helping."

He laughed again, loving every second of her fluster. She paused at the door, turned, and reached up to kiss him lightly.

"I'll see you tonight," she said, softer now.

"You better," he murmured, his thumb brushing her cheek.

And with that, she slipped out the door—heart still racing, smile still lingering.

He stood there for a second, running a hand through his hair, a slow smile tugging at his lips.

And then he walked back to the bedroom, reaching for his phone.

***

CHAPTER TWENTY TWO

THE STORM HITS

Angad stood at the door longer than necessary, watching the spot where Reva had disappeared moments ago. The hallway was quiet now, but her presence still lingered—in the warmth on his skin, in the faint scent of her clinging to his shirt, in the echo of her laughter bouncing somewhere in his head.

He felt… light.

Too light.

As if something had shifted and made room inside him for more.

He turned slowly and walked back into the bedroom, a small smile playing at the corners of his mouth—until he picked up his phone.

And stilled.

Six missed calls.

Naina (4), Lata (2)

His breath caught. Guilt crashed over him like a tidal wave.

The timestamp hit him like a punch—during breakfast. And before that.

When he was—

Shit.

His throat went dry.

He had never missed a call from the kids. Not once. Not in all these years of raising them alone. He'd taken calls during board meetings, from bathrooms, and in the middle of interviews. Because *they* came first. Always.

His grip on the phone tightened.

He imagined Anika's small voice asking where he was. Avik holding out the phone to Naina, hoping someone else could try. The thought made his stomach turn. He couldn't even picture their faces at that moment—it hurt too much.

He had failed.

He had let down the very people he swore to protect, to prioritize, to build his world around.

And for what?

For a woman who made him forget it all.

For a night where desire drowned out reason—where the only thing louder than their ragged breaths was the sound of his own defenses shattering.

For want.

For weakness.

For himself.

That was the part that gutted him.

He had allowed himself to feel good again.

To be touched. To be seen. To be someone other than just *Dad.*

And in the process, he had slipped.

The worst part? It hadn't even occurred to him that something might be wrong. He hadn't noticed the silence of his phone. He hadn't listened for it.

He had been... happy.

He sat on the edge of the bed, the weight of that happiness now settling like stones in his chest. He didn't deserve it. Not if it came at their expense.

She had done nothing wrong. This was on him.

Still—what the hell was he doing?

Letting her in. Letting this happen. Letting himself believe that he could have *more.*

Opening the door to her meant opening the door to everything he had locked away—love, intimacy, the vulnerability of sharing a life. He hadn't shut the world out to suffer in silence. He had done it for them—for his kids. To keep their world whole. To keep their *father* standing.

His fingers hovered over Reva's name. For a moment, he wanted to hear her voice again. To cling to the softness she'd left behind in this room. To go back ten minutes before the guilt set in.

Instead, he opened their message thread.

'Something came up. Can't do dinner tonight.'

He stared at the words. It was a lie. But he told himself it was necessary.

The moment he hit *send*, Angad's phone rang again.

Naina.

He didn't hesitate this time. He swiped to answer and brought the phone to his ear. "Aunty—what happened?"

"Angad," her voice was tight with strain but calm, trying not to alarm him further, "We've been trying to reach you since morning."

"I saw. I'm sorry. I—" His voice cracked. "What happened? Is everything okay?"

"It is now. But Avik fell while chasing the ball in the garden. Scraped his knee, hit his chin. Nothing serious, but he bled a little and got scared. Anika panicked, too."

Angad shot to his feet, heart racing. "Oh, God. And I wasn't…"

"They were crying for you," Naina continued gently. "Especially Avik. He kept saying, 'Call Daddy. He always picks up.'"

She paused. "And when you didn't, it only scared them more."

Angad shut his eyes. His chest burned with guilt.

"I—I should've been there."

"It's okay now, *beta*. He's been cleaned up and bandaged. They're fine, Angad. Just shaken. They're resting."

"I want to talk to them," he said quickly. "Please."

A second later, the video call switched on. The screen wobbled before showing Avik, his eyes red from crying, and a small bandage on his chin. Anika sat beside him, clinging to his arm.

"Daddy…" Avik's voice was small, uncertain.

"I'm here, buddy," Angad said, his voice thick. "I'm sorry. I'm so, so sorry I didn't answer. Are you okay?"

Avik nodded slowly. "I fell. It hurt. You weren't there."

Angad's heart split open. He looked helplessly at the screen. "I should've been. I should've picked up. I promise I'll never miss your call again, champ. Never."

Anika looked at him, eyes shining with unshed tears. "You always pick up, Daddy. Why didn't you today?"

He didn't have an answer.

The silence hung like a noose.

Naina gently took the phone. Her voice was calm, soothing. "Angad, he's okay now. It was just a scraped knee, a bit of shock. These things happen."

He ran a hand through his hair, guilt pressing down on him like a weight. "I should've been there. I've *always* been there."

Raj's voice came in, firm but kind, as he took the phone from Naina. "You're still there, *beta*. You always will be. One missed call doesn't make you a bad father."

"But he was crying for me," Angad whispered.

"And he'll forget about the pain by tomorrow," Raj said gently. "But what he *won't* forget is the love you've surrounded him with every day of his life. One incident doesn't undo all of that."

Naina's voice returned, softer now. "They're tired. I'll put them to nap. We'll be back home tomorrow."

He nodded mutely, swallowing back the storm inside him. "Thanks, Aunty."

After the call ended, Angad sat frozen on the edge of the bed, staring at nothing.

The soft sheets still held the scent of Reva.

*

Reva was unlocking her apartment door when her phone buzzed in her hand. She glanced at the screen, expecting something sweet from Angad.

Angad: *Something came up. Can't do dinner tonight.*

She stilled. The smile that had lingered since morning slipped from her face.

That didn't sound like him. Not after last night. Not after this morning.

Her fingers moved quickly.

Reva: *Everything okay? Want to talk?*

No reply.

A knot began forming in her chest. She tapped open her call log.

Two missed calls from Maa.

Her pulse jumped. She hit redial immediately.

Naina picked up on the first ring.

"Maa? Everything okay?"

There was a pause, soft rustling on the other end. "Yes, *beta*. Now it is. But Avik had a small accident in the garden this morning. He fell and bruised his chin and scraped his knee. Nothing serious—just a bit shaken. They called Angad, but he didn't answer. I tried you, too."

Reva's breath caught. She sank down onto the edge of her sofa, her mind racing. Her phone had been on silent. She hadn't even looked at it until now.

"Oh God. I didn't see the calls—Maa, I'm so sorry."

"I figured you might still be asleep," Naina said gently, her tone uncharacteristically knowing. "After all, you had such a late night last night. We thought both you and Angad would be sleeping in."

Reva's breath hitched. Her cheeks flushed hot. "What—what do you mean, Maa?"

There was a beat of silence, then Naina chuckled softly. "The launch event, Reva. The party? That was last night, wasn't it? How did it go?"

Relief surged through Reva so fast it almost made her dizzy.

"Oh… yeah. Yes, it was good. Really good, actually. A great turnout."

She rubbed her forehead, pushing away the flash of panic that had momentarily taken over. "Umm… have you spoken to Angad yet?"

"Yeah, just now. Spoke to the kids. He was really upset… felt terrible for not answering earlier."

Reva closed her eyes, her chest tightening with guilt. She could picture him now—his face, drawn with worry and self-reproach. The way he must've looked when he realized he'd missed the calls.

She hadn't heard hers either. They'd both been too wrapped up in each other. Too consumed.

Too distracted.

"I'm going to him," she said suddenly.

"Reva…" Naina's voice was calm, measured, "Give him a little time. He's still processing it."

"Hmm..." Reva murmured, already halfway to her room.

She ended the call and moved on autopilot—straight to the shower, her thoughts in a spin. She dressed quickly, pulling on a comfortable sundress.

She had to see him. Had to let him know he wasn't alone in this.

They were in this together—even the messy, guilt-ridden, complicated parts.

*

The short walk to his building felt longer than usual. Each step carried a growing heaviness in her chest. How do you apologize for something you didn't mean to do—but felt entirely responsible for? Reva didn't know what she'd say, only that she needed to say something. Needed to see him. Needed to know that he—*they*—were okay.

She rang the bell.

No answer.

She hesitated, then rang it again. The silence on the other side felt louder this time.

Finally, the door opened.

Angad stood there, his face shadowed, shoulders stiff, eyes tired—he wasn't the man who had kissed her breathless just hours ago. Something in him had folded inward. Tight. Guarded.

"Hey…" she said softly, searching his face.

He didn't respond at first. Just looked at her. No warmth. No anger, either. Just… exhaustion.

"I just spoke to Maa," she began. "She told me about Avik. I…"

"You shouldn't have come," he interrupted, his tone low and tightly controlled, emotion buried just beneath the surface.

The words stung, but she didn't back away. "I just wanted to check on you. The kids..."

"They're fine now," he replied, stepping back slightly, only enough to let her in. "Bandaged up. Safe."

"Then what's this tone, Angad?" Her voice cracked, but she held her ground. "Why does it feel like you are shutting me out?"

He looked away, jaw tense. "Because I can't afford this."

Reva blinked. "Can't afford what?"

"I missed six calls, Reva. I never miss even one. Not from them."

"I know," she said, her voice barely above a whisper. "I missed mine, too."

He looked away, jaw tight. "That's the problem. We were both so... out of it. I can't afford that, Reva. Not as a father. Avik was crying. Looking for me. And I was…"

His words trailed off, but the weight of them hung in the air between them.

Reva stepped closer, hesitant. "Angad, we're human. It was one morning. You've been an incredible father. This doesn't erase that."

He didn't move, didn't speak.

"I get it," she added quietly. "You're scared. You've built your entire world around not letting them feel abandoned. But they're safe. They're loved. They'll understand."

"No, Reva. That's not how it works. Not with them. Not with me." His voice broke slightly. "I've been *everything* for them since the day they were born. They don't get to have me on and off. I don't get to check in and out of being their father. They are my world. For the past five and a half years, I've made every decision in my life based on them. Every choice. Every routine. And the one time they needed me—really needed me—I wasn't there. I was… distracted."

Reva swallowed, something sinking in her chest. "So… you're saying I'm a distraction?"

"I'm saying I can't afford to be that man. The one who forgets the world when he's with you."

For a moment, silence. The apartment was quiet, dim, the warmth from just this morning missing. She stood near the edge of the sofa, unsure. He stood by the window, arms crossed.

"I didn't come to defend what happened," she said finally. "I came because I feel just as awful. I missed the calls, too…"

He looked back at her finally, eyes tired. Hurt.

"I'm sorry. I can't let this happen again."

Reva felt the words like a slap, not because they were cruel—but because they were final. Protective. Distant.

He was shutting her out to protect what mattered most to him.

"I should go," she said quietly, swallowing the knot in her throat.

He nodded once, almost mechanically.

As she turned to leave, Reva's steps were steady—but her chest felt hollow. The closeness of the morning now felt like a distant dream, blurred by reality. Rejection mixed with guilt swirled in her like a bitter brew.

Maybe this was a mistake, her heart whispered. Maybe she wasn't cut out for a life already filled with responsibility, with love that had to be earned every single day.

Maybe wanting him had been selfish.

Angad watched her retreating figure, a part of him screaming to call her back—while another part, louder, heavier, told him this was for the best.

And yet, even as the door clicked shut behind her, the ache in his chest told him he might've just pushed away the one thing he never knew he needed.

***

CHAPTER TWENTY THREE

AFTER SHOCKS

The airport arrivals area buzzed with familiar chaos—luggage wheels clattering against the tiled floor, families reuniting in tearful embraces, overhead announcements echoing in clipped tones. But Angad didn't hear any of it. He stood still, eyes scanning past the automatic glass doors, blocking out everything else.

He hadn't slept properly the night before. The apartment was quieter than usual. Angad had paced through the rooms restlessly, unable to shake off the image of Reva's eyes right before she left. Hurt, confused, rejected.

He'd told himself he needed space—for the kids, for his guilt, for everything he'd screwed up in the past 24 hours. But then, in the silence of the house, all he could feel was her absence.

Reva had messaged once.

'I'm sorry, too. For everything.'

And he hadn't replied. Yet.

Between the kids' video call and the way Reva had left, his head had been spinning. He didn't even know what he would say to them. He just knew he needed to see their faces.

Just then, a movement to his left caught his eye. Ramesh — the Khannas' longtime driver — was weaving his way through the crowd, craning his neck toward him. Angad straightened instinctively, his eyes flicking behind the older man.

But there was no Reva.

A twinge of disappointment cut through, sharp and silent.

His jaw clenched. He had told her to leave. Had shut her out. And she had listened. She didn't come.

He shifted on his feet and exhaled slowly, just as the glass doors slid open again—his gaze zeroed in on two small figures bounding toward him with uncontainable energy.

"Daddy!"

"Daadddyyyy!"

His heart twisted at the sound of their voices.

Anika reached him first, barreling into his arms with enough force to nearly knock him back. Avik was right behind, his backpack slipping off one shoulder as he threw himself at his father's side. Angad dropped to his knees, wrapping them both in a fierce embrace, burying his face into their warm, familiar necks. They smelled like travel—scented wipes, hand sanitizer, and the faint sweetness of chocolate milk.

"I missed you two like crazy," he whispered, pressing kisses to their hair, one after the other. "Every single minute."

"We missed you, too, Daddy," they said together, clinging to him like he was their entire world.

He shifted slightly to face Avik, gently brushing a finger over the small white bandage on his chin and then glancing down at the cartoon-covered plaster on his knee.

"You okay, champ?" he asked softly.

Avik beamed. "It doesn't hurt anymore! See?" He stuck his leg out proudly. "It's Scooby-Doo!"

Angad smiled and pulled him into another quick hug. "Of course it is. You must be the bravest boy in the whole world. How was the flight?"

Behind them, Raj caught up, slightly breathless from running after the kids.

"The flight was smooth," Raj said, adjusting his collar. "They slept most of the way. Played some games. Ate a lot of cookies."

"Thank you, Raj Uncle. Naina Aunty." Angad stood up as Naina approached with Lata and the luggage in tow. He offered a small smile. "I hope they weren't too much to handle."

"They were absolute angels," Naina replied, pulling Angad into a warm hug. "And don't let them convince you otherwise."

Just then, Anika tugged at his hand. He scooped her up without a thought, her arms wrapping tightly around his neck. Her little face was scrunched into a thoughtful frown.

"Where's Reedi?"

Angad blinked. "What?"

"Reedi," Anika said again, her tone bordering on accusatory. "She said she'd come with you to pick us up."

"When did she say that?" he asked carefully, trying to keep his voice steady.

"Yesterday," Anika said, thinking hard. "Or maybe the day before. She said she'd be there when we landed."

"And we'll go for dinner. You promised," Avik chimed in, tugging at the hand he was holding.

"You pinky-promised! We'd all have dinner together. You, me, Avik, and Reedi," Anika reminded him.

Angad's throat tightened. His mind flashed back to that evening at the restaurant—the laughter, Reva's soft smile, the warmth of hope blooming quietly in his chest.

"You did," Avik insisted, wide-eyed. "That night. When we were flying, and you and Reedi had that fancy dinner."

"I did," he admitted, his voice quiet. Of course, they remembered. Of course, *he* remembered.

"So where is she?" Anika asked again, brow creasing. "She said she'd come."

Angad looked down at their hopeful faces, his chest clenching painfully.

He had promised.

And now—what? Reva was gone. Or worse, he'd pushed her away.

"She... she had to work today," he said as he put Anika down, hating the words even as they left his mouth. "Something important came up last minute."

"But she knew we were coming," Anika murmured, still unconvinced.

"I know," Angad said gently, wrapping an arm around each of them. "And I promise—" his voice faltered for half a second, "—we'll talk to her soon, okay?"

The twins exchanged a skeptical look.

Avik glanced up at him. "We can still have dinner, right? All of us? Maybe tomorrow?"

Angad hesitated. "We'll see," he said softly, brushing his hair back. "Let's get you both home first, hmm?"

As they began to walk toward the exit, Angad and the kids turned back toward the Khannas. He gave them a respectful smile, and Avik quickly bent down to touch Naina and Raj's feet. Angad followed suit, murmuring a quiet "thank you" and "take care."

Anika waved brightly. "Bye, Nani! Bye, Nanu! Bye, Ramesh bhaiya!"

The Khannas smiled and waved them off warmly.

Lata, standing patiently with their bags near the parked car, stepped forward as they approached. Angad ruffled the kids' hair again and opened the car door, still replaying that one question in his mind.

Where's Reedi?

*

The scent of slow-cooked onions and garlic filled the Khannas' kitchen, but Reva barely noticed. Her hands moved mechanically—adding spices, stirring, tasting, adjusting. She had offered to cook lunch for her parents before they returned from the airport, but now that she was here, the task felt distant—like she moved with practiced ease, her body going through the motions while her mind drifted elsewhere. She didn't feel present. Not really.

All she could see was Angad's face from yesterday.

That moment when she stood in his doorway, heart in her throat, trying to find the words to say she was there for him. With him. With *them*. And the way he'd stepped back—not to let her in, but to quietly retreat into himself.

That look in his eyes.

Guilt. Panic. Distance.

And then: the quietest rejection.

"I should go," she had said.

He didn't stop her.

She closed her eyes, ladle hovering above the pot. Her chest still felt hollow. Not just bruised—vacant. Like something had been gently, deliberately taken out of her.

She had fallen for him. Entirely. Angad, with his brooding intensity and quiet humor. The twins, with their mismatched shoes and secret whispers. It had all crept in slowly, then taken over all at once.

And now… nothing.

She wouldn't chase him. *She couldn't.* Not after the silence that followed. Not after the look in his eyes, so carefully blank, it hurt. He wasn't ready. Or maybe he didn't want her tangled up in his already-complicated world.

Her phone buzzed on the counter. She didn't even glance at it.

Instead, she turned off the stove and wiped her hands on a dish towel, then walked out to the small balcony. From there, she could see the society's play area below—alive with kids shrieking, splashing in the pool, chasing each other across the lawns. It was a typical Sunday, full of life and noise. But she couldn't hear any of it—not really. Her mind was too loud, drowning everything out with the echoes of yesterday.

She heard the familiar rumble of the elevator and the thump of suitcase wheels in the corridor. Her parents were back.

Reva smoothed her kurta, blinked once, and went to open the door.

"Welcome home," she said, pasting on a smile as Raj and Naina walked in, looking mildly travel-worn but happy. "Lunch is ready."

Naina pulled her into a hug. "We missed you."

"Missed you too," Reva said softly, glancing over their shoulders for just a moment. It was only Ramesh, following in with the suitcases.

No tiny sneakers. No excited twin voices. No tall frame with that familiar quiet presence.

Just her parents.

"You're looking for them," Naina said as she removed her dupatta and set down her handbag.

Reva blinked. "No—I just thought maybe Angad—"

"He took them home. They needed some time together—just the three of them," Raj said, making his way to the wash basin. "You should've seen it… the way they ran into his arms like little rockets. And the way he held them—like someone had just put his heart back together."

Reva froze mid-step, her breath catching. A sharp, unspoken ache bloomed in her chest. She could picture it—Angad dropping to his knees, arms open, the kids racing into his embrace. That fierce, protective love in his eyes. The kind of reunion that mended cracks invisible to the world.

She swallowed hard, blinking rapidly.

"I see," she murmured, forcing her voice to stay even. "That's good. They needed that."

Raj turned off the tap, drying his hands slowly, eyes flicking toward her. "They asked about you, you know."

Her heart gave a painful lurch. "They did?"

He nodded. "At the airport. Anika looked around the terminal like she expected you to pop out of the crowd. Avik was showing off his Scooby Doo bandage."

Her throat tightened. "Is he okay now?"

"Completely fine. Barely a scratch. But Angad… he looked exhausted. And shaken."

Reva's brows drew together. "What happened?"

"He was late answering his phone. Felt like he let them down." Raj's voice softened. "He didn't."

Reva didn't reply. She busied herself setting out the plates, though her hands shook slightly.

"Why didn't you come to the airport?" Naina asked as they sat down. "They were really hoping you would."

Reva looked down at her hands, still damp from the sink, her fingers trembling slightly. "I had work," she said quietly. "I'll call them later. Besides, I—I figured they'd want time with their father. I didn't want to intrude."

Raj gave her a long look. "You weren't intruding, Reva. You were part of their little world, too. Like it or not."

She didn't answer. Couldn't.

Because part of her *wanted* that to be true. Wanted it too much.

But Angad had made his choice, hadn't he?

He'd sent her away—not cruelly, not angrily—but with a quiet finality that stung more than rage ever could.

"How's Sanaya?" she asked, changing the subject. "And Mumbai? Was it manageable?"

"It was hectic," Raj answered with a sigh. "Sanaya loved having the twins over, showing off her home and her city. We did all the touristy stuff. Avik's fall was the only scare."

Reva immediately straightened. "How bad was it?"

Naina shook her head. "Not bad at all. Just a scrape on the chin and a bruised knee. More dramatic than dangerous. But Angad looked shaken. I think he still felt guilty for not picking up the call."

Reva looked away, her heart tugging painfully. *She should have been there. For Avik. For all of them.*

A beat of silence passed. Then, "The food smells amazing," Raj said gently.

"Thanks," Reva murmured.

But her appetite had disappeared.

*

"We made a glitter card for Reedi!" Avik said proudly as they entered the home. "It's in my backpack. Can we give it to her now?"

Angad's throat went dry. "Maybe… maybe you can give it to her another day."

Anika's voice dropped. "Is she mad at us?"

"No!" he said quickly. "No, of course not. Nothing like that."

Neither of them replied.

Anika, who had insisted on being carried all the way from the parking lot to their apartment, simply rested her head on his shoulder.

Avik slipped his small hand into Angad's.

The twins soon launched into excited chatter, recounting stories from Mumbai—the beach, the Chowpatty, the boat ride. Their words tumbled over one another in a blur of memories and laughter.

Angad listened. He nodded, smiled at the right places, asked questions, and even laughed a little.

But his mind was elsewhere.

On Reva.

On what he'd walked away from.

He had told himself he was doing the right thing—protecting the kids, shielding their fragile world from the chaos of his own heart.

But if pulling away had hurt them, too... then what exactly was he protecting anymore?

Later that night, long after the twins had drifted off—Avik clutching his Dino soft toy and Anika curled up with her blanket tucked beneath her chin—Angad sat alone in his bedroom, the silence pressing in around him.

The glow of his phone screen cast a soft light on his face.

Reva's message was still there.

I'm sorry, too. For everything.

Just one sentence. Simple. Heavy.

His thumb hovered over it as if a reply would somehow unlock what he didn't yet have the courage to face.

But the words wouldn't come.

Instead, his mind betrayed him, drifting to her. The feel of her in his arms. The way she had melted against him that night, like her body finally exhaled in his touch—like she belonged there.

The taste of her lips still lingered—soft, warm, unforgettable. The way her fingers had fisted in his shirt. The way she'd whispered his name as if it were something sacred.

She'd looked so alive in that moment. So open. So his.

And now… she was gone. A breath away and yet unreachable.

He leaned back against the bed, scrubbing a hand down his face.

What had he done?

He had pushed her away to protect the only constants in his life—his children. But in doing so, had he carved out something vital from his own heart?

She was chaos and comfort all at once. She saw him—the man behind the dad, behind the businessman. And God, she loved the kids like they were her own.

But that was the thing, wasn't it?

She deserved a life of her own. Not just one where she mothered *his* kids.

What if, one day, she wanted a child of her own? A family built from the start—not picked up mid-story with scars and baggage he couldn't ever erase?

He couldn't give her that. Not without rewriting everything.

And he couldn't be selfish. Not with someone like Reva. Not her.

She deserved lightness. Freedom.

A man whose life wasn't already spoken for.

Not someone like him—who wore responsibility like a second skin, whose time and heart were already divided.

Reva deserved more.

More than fleeting moments and half-measures.

More than what he could ever give her.

Much more than him.

Angad looked down at his phone again.

Still, no reply came to his mind.

Because what could he possibly say that would undo the damage?

That he'd made a mistake?

That he missed her voice?

His jaw clenched. This wasn't just guilt. It was an ache. A hollow ache that echoed louder every night she wasn't there.

Angad set the phone face down on the side table, exhaling sharply.

He wasn't ready to reply.

Not yet.

***

CHAPTER TWENTY FOUR

TANGLED THREADS

The days crept by in silken threads of unease and longing.

Reva kept herself busy—busier than necessary. Her work schedule was suddenly packed, her calendar flooded with tasks she didn't remember agreeing to. But even in the middle of emails, edits, or client calls, her thoughts drifted… always back to them.

She saw the twins now and then—at school during pickup, once when they came up to Naina's for *rajma-chawal* and stayed to finish an entire bar of chocolate she'd left in the fridge, and a couple of times at the clubhouse when she was too exhausted to say no to their grins.

Each hug left her a little more unraveled.

Each *"Reedi!"* tugged at something deep inside her.

She was smiling, laughing even—but every moment without them, without *him*, quietly hollowed out a space inside her she couldn't ignore.

One evening, they dashed into the clubhouse after a swim, dripping water and laughter. Reva helped them towel off, brushing Avik's wet hair back and redoing Anika's ponytail.

"Did you eat enough lunch today?" she asked, straightening Anika's T-shirt.

"Uh-huh," Anika nodded. "Raju Bhaiya made spaghetti with red sauce."

"Daddy ate with us!" Avik chimed in proudly.

At the mention of him, Reva looked up instinctively. Her voice came out lighter than she felt. "And how is your dad?"

Avik nodded. "Always talking on the phone. Or typing."

Anika watched her carefully, her brows scrunched in confusion. "Did you and daddy have a fight?"

The question landed like a soft punch to the gut.

Reva blinked. "What? No, sweetheart. Why would you think that?"

"Because… you didn't come for dinner," Anika said softly. "You promised."

"I know." Reva tried to keep her voice even. "I wanted to, really. But something came up at work. Lots of deadlines. I'm sorry, my darlings."

Anika leaned in to hug her. "We're not mad. But next time, no work, okay?"

Reva pressed a kiss to the top of her head, her heart heavy with guilt and love all tangled together. "Okay, sweetie. Next time, no work."

And maybe—just maybe—no more lies.

*

For Angad, the days that followed stretched long and strange.

The twins fell back into their usual routine, their laughter and constant chatter filling up the silences around him—but one silence still echoed louder than all the rest.

Reva's.

She had quietly withdrawn from the little spaces she once filled in his life.

He knew she still saw the kids now and then—but with him, she'd gone completely silent. Their work project was done, and the website was launched. There was no reason for her to come to his office anymore. If anything came up, she handled it remotely—efficient, distant, professional.

She skipped dinners at the Khannas' when he was there. And while Naina always had a ready excuse—"She had a client call," or "She wasn't feeling well"—Angad saw through it.

Reva was avoiding him.

And she was only honoring the distance *he* had created.

He'd drawn the line that day, and she walked away. He told himself it was the right thing—that she deserved more than the chaos of his life, more than slivers of time or attention from a man who could never fully show up for her. She needed someone who came with a clean slate.

Not him. Not his baggage.

So he let her go.

But every time the twins mentioned her—usually casually, like it wasn't the center of his universe—something inside him clenched.

"We saw Reedi at school today!"

"She gave me a new sticker book!"

"She made us *rajma-chawal* when we went to Nani's! They were as good as Nani makes."

He'd always ask: *"How's she doing?"*

And they'd respond with innocent nods or details like *"She was wearing blue"* or *"She said she had a big project."* Never the answer he really needed.

One night, while tucking the kids into bed, Avik looked up at him with wide, questioning eyes.

"Daddy… did you and Reedi fight?"

The words cut deep, catching him off guard.

He smoothed his son's hair and replied gently, "No, champ. We're just both really busy."

Avik gave him a solemn nod, as if he understood the gravity of the deadlines. "Reedi said the same thing."

"The same thing?" Angad asked gently.

"Yeah," Anika answered. "She said you both are just really busy. That's why the dinner didn't happen."

His smile faltered just a little before he quickly masked it. "Well, then. Looks like both of us are terrible at keeping promises, hmm? I'm sorry."

They were mirroring each other without even realizing it.

Or maybe that was the worst part—they both realized it all too well.

She wasn't there because *he* had built a wall. And she wasn't the kind of woman who begged to be let back in.

And still… he missed her. *God, he missed her.*

He missed her laugh during dinners at her parents' home—the way it used to light up even the dullest conversations.

He missed her at work—her voice gently correcting his sentence mid-presentation, the way she winced when she sipped his black coffee instead of her cappuccino.

He missed her at home—her presence woven into his sheets, limbs tangled with his, soft breath against his neck.

He missed her touch, her kisses, the way she looked that morning, asleep in his bed—like she belonged there. Like he wanted her to.

He told himself he didn't regret it. That he had done the right thing.

But every night, when the house went quiet, and he was left alone with nothing but the hum of his thoughts, one truth refused to loosen its grip:

He hadn't protected her from heartbreak.

He had simply broken her himself.

*

It was a quiet Friday evening. Reva had just wrapped up work and was unwinding in her favorite corner of the clubhouse—the far end by the large bay windows that overlooked the kids' play area. A soft breeze filtered in through the glass panels, bringing with it the distant, happy shrieks of children chasing each other.

The twins were darting in and out of the padded tunnels and mini-obstacle course. Avik, Anika, and a few other kids were squealing with delight, dodging behind the slides. Their laughter echoed in waves, making Reva smile faintly, even as her eyes drifted over the pages of a magazine she wasn't truly reading.

A few feet away, Lata's phone rang. The older woman stepped aside to take the call. It was meant to be a short one—just a check-in with her family in the village—but moments later, Reva caught the sudden change in her tone. Her voice cracked, and her words became hushed, trembling with urgency.

Reva immediately sat up. "Lata *didi*? What's wrong?"

Lata ended the call, her eyes glassy. "It's my mother," she whispered, visibly shaken. "She just had a stroke... my brother called. They don't think she'll last long. They're calling me. I—I need to go."

Without a second thought, Reva rose. "Don't worry. Just get your things. Give me the details of where you have to go, and let me book your tickets."

"But the kids—Angad Sir—" Lata's voice was strained, even as she gave Reva her address. "I can't just leave them like this."

"You're not. Don't worry about them. I'll be there with the kids," Reva said softly. "Just call him and explain everything. I'm sure he'll be okay with it. Just focus on getting to your mother."

Within minutes, Reva had arranged her train tickets and called Ramesh, asking him to come to Angad's building and take Lata to the station. As she reassured the children and collected their belongings, Lata stepped aside again—this time to make a call to Angad.

*

Angad was still at work, staring at an overflowing inbox, when his phone buzzed. Seeing Lata's name, he answered immediately.

"Hello?"

"Sir…" Lata's voice cracked. "I—I'm sorry to call you at work. My mother, in the village… she's very sick. I've just been told to come as soon as I can."

He sat up straighter, instantly alert. "Are the kids okay?"

"Yes, yes, they're with Reva Madam. She was at the clubhouse, and she said not to worry... that she would take care of everything. She even booked my ticket." Lata's words rushed out, choked with emotion. "I didn't know what to do, Sir. I'm so sorry for leaving like this."

"Don't apologize," Angad said firmly. "You need to be with your family right now. Go take care of your mother. I'll handle everything here."

"Sir, I—I don't even have enough cash for the travel—"

"I'll send some money to your UPI account right now," he cut in gently. "And I'll ask Mohan to drop you at the station."

Lata broke into quiet sobs on the line, murmuring her gratitude. "Thank you, Sir… thank you. Don't send Mohan. Reva Madam has already called Ramesh."

Once the call ended, Angad sat back in his chair, staring at the phone for a long moment. Reva. She didn't have to step in. She had no obligation. Yet, she was there—for his children, for Lata, for him… again.

He didn't know what he'd say when he saw her.

But he couldn't stop thinking about it.

*

Lata left with a promise to call once she reached her village, just as Reva and the kids arrived at the apartment.

Reva paused at the door.

The familiarity of the place hit her like a wave—the faint scent of sandalwood from the diffuser by the entryway, the gentle hum of the air conditioning, the quiet. Everything was the same… and yet, nothing was.

She hadn't set foot in the apartment since that day.

The memories surged back—waking up tangled in Angad's sheets, the quiet clatter of him moving around the kitchen, the warmth of borrowed clothes against her skin as she slipped out in his tee and shorts, heels clicking beneath the absurdity of it all.

And then… the silence.

The sting of rejection.

The hollow that bloomed in her chest as she walked away—uninvited, unwanted, unsure if she'd ever be welcome again.

Her fingers instinctively tightened around Avik's as he fumbled with his water bottle. She swallowed hard, bracing herself.

Although they were sad to see Lata go, the twins were practically buzzing with excitement to have Reva back in their home. Avik clung to her hand while Anika skipped ahead, chattering about what they could watch on TV.

"Come on, *bachche*," she said softly. "Shoes off at the door."

Anika dropped her backpack with a sigh of relief, kicking off her sneakers. "Can we watch something before dinner?"

Reva nodded, managing a small smile. "Half an hour, max. Then we eat."

They scrambled to the couch with practiced ease, grabbing the remote, already arguing about which episode of their favorite cartoon to play.

She moved quietly into the kitchen, where Raju had already prepared the twins' favorite—mac and cheese. The aroma was warm and familiar, almost comforting. Reva lifted the lid, gave it a thoughtful stir, and then added a generous handful of grated cheese and a sprinkle of dried herbs to make it extra creamy—just the way she knew they'd like it.

She'd never cooked here before. The only meal she'd ever had in this kitchen was that quiet breakfast Angad had made—coffee, toast, and stolen glances. And yet, her hands moved as if they knew the space. As if her presence had once been etched into its corners, waiting to be resumed.

The way the cutlery drawer stuck slightly, the cabinet with the kid-sized plates—it all came to her with unnerving ease.

It unsettled her—how familiar this unfamiliarity felt.

She didn't belong here.

She had to keep reminding herself of that.

But then Avik came dashing in, arms looping tightly around her waist just as she was reaching for a serving spoon. "It smells so nice, Reedi," he said, his face tilted up, eyes shining.

Her throat tightened, and she ruffled his hair gently, hiding the sudden sting behind her smile. "Wait till you taste it, mister. Go wash up, I'm about to serve."

*

Angad left the office minutes after he hung up the call with Lata. She will be gone by the time he reaches home.

And Reva... Reva was home with the kids.

He hadn't seen her since that afternoon when she walked out of his apartment.

He hadn't heard her voice.

Hadn't caught that quiet trail of floral and vanilla that used to follow her like a secret.

He unlocked the door with a tight breath, half-ready for chaos, half-bracing for the sight of her.

What he wasn't prepared for—was the sound of Reva's laughter ringing down the hallway. So familiar. So easy.

It hit him square in the chest. He stepped inside and froze. Lights spilled warm across the floor. Voices floated from the living room.

And at the center of it all, he saw her—Reva. Curled on the rug between the twins, a blanket draped across her legs, book in hand. Her hair was loose, falling over one shoulder as she read. Her voice dropped into a whisper for effect, and Anika giggled, eyes wide. Avik clutched a stuffed toy in one hand and a spoonful of dessert in the other.

He didn't move. The sight punched the air out of his lungs.

Reva looked up, her smile freezing when their eyes met.

The silence that fell was thick—weeks of unsaid things pressed between them.

"I was just—" she began, rising to her feet.

"Daddy!" Anika called out, running to him. "We had dinner and story time. Lata Aunty had to go see her Mumma. Reedi came home with us!"

"She read the one with the monster and the jellybeans," Avik added, grinning. "And she made the best mac and cheese, but made us eat the vegetables first."

Angad's gaze lifted from the twins to the woman behind them. She rose slowly from the cozy sprawl she'd shared with the kids as if reluctant to break the moment—aware, perhaps, that everything would shift now that he was home.

Reva.

Her hair was loose, her soft orange dress highlighted her curves, and her feet were bare on the marble floor—like she belonged. Like she'd never left.

And yet, every cell in his body remembered that she had.

She stood there with a soft smile, hands unconsciously fidgeting. Eyes meeting his briefly… then darting away.

He couldn't speak.

"Daddy!" Anika tugged his hand, impatient. "You didn't hear? Reedi made us eat vegetables."

"And then gave us double cheese!" Avik added proudly. "But only *after* we promised to brush properly tonight."

Still, Angad said nothing. Couldn't. His heart was thudding too loudly in his chest.

Reva finally cleared her throat and spoke—calm, careful. "Lata *didi* left as we got here. She promised to call when she reaches. I, uh… figured it was easier if the kids came home. They were tired."

Her voice wasn't sharp. It wasn't warm either. Just neutral. Too neutral.

"Thanks," Angad managed, his throat dry. "For stepping in."

She nodded, already turning toward the kitchen as if she hadn't just cracked him open with that one moment of eye contact.

He watched her move—unhurried, composed. The weight of her presence hit him harder than he expected. Not just because she was here but because of how deeply he'd missed *this*. Her. The ease with which she fit into their home. Into his life.

Into him.

***

CHAPTER TWENTY FIVE

THE SPACE IN BETWEEN

Angad settled onto the couch, the twins climbing into their usual spots—Anika curling up beside him, Avik perched on the armrest like a little king surveying his kingdom.

They started telling him about their day in bits and bursts—how Avik had been "it" during tag, how Reva had made them eat *all* their vegetables before giving them cheesy mac, how she let them watch an episode of their favorite show before dinner. He listened quietly, a soft smile tugging at the corner of his lips, though his mind wasn't entirely with their words.

From the corner of his eye, he watched her.

Reva moved to the kitchen, speaking to Raju in that calm, competent tone he knew too well. "Let's keep it simple, Raju. French toast, some fruit, and if the kids want something else, we'll figure it out in the morning." She opened a cabinet, checked the bread supply, then moved to the fridge.

It was like watching something that had always belonged finally fall into place. She moved through his kitchen like she'd lived there all along—calm, sure, quietly capable. She hadn't done this before, hadn't played this role in this space… and yet, it didn't feel new or wrong. It felt just right.

She didn't ask where things were. She didn't hesitate.

She just... fit. In their home. In their routine. In their lives.

And it rattled him more than he cared to admit.

"I'm going to change," he said aloud, mostly to the room, partly to himself. He stood and walked off to his bedroom, the silence from Reva echoing louder than any answer.

When he returned, dressed in a T-shirt and pajamas, he found all three of them in the living room again—Avik and Anika in a heated debate over what show to watch, Reva lounging on the floor cushions, legs tucked under her, looking more like herself than he'd seen in weeks.

Something about the scene hit him square in the chest.

She belonged here.

And yet, she didn't.

"Okay, kids, time for bed now. I also have to go home," she said softly as the cartoon ended, catching his glance.

"Nooo!" Anika cried. "One more story!"

"Please, Reedi," Avik chimed in. "You said weekend means we can stay up late."

"You *already* stayed up late," she teased gently, but her smile was touched with affection.

Their little hands reached out, pulling her back.

Anika immediately whined, "But you promised another story!"

"That was before you demanded twenty more minutes of TV," Reva replied, trying to sound stern but failing.

Avik, ever the negotiator, jumped in. "Please, Reedi? Just one more story. Then promise we'll sleep."

"And you'll brush your teeth properly?" she countered, arching an eyebrow.

Two enthusiastic nods followed.

Reva hesitated, her smile faltering for the briefest moment.

She looked up—and found his gaze already on her. Steady. Unspoken. Something passed between them in that stillness.

Then Angad nodded, his voice quiet but certain. "Stay."

Her heart stuttered, but she kept her tone light. "Okay," she said, turning to the kids. "But first—teeth brushed, nightwear on, and *then* story time. Deal?"

"YAAAY!" the twins chorused, jumping up and darting toward their room in a flurry of giggles and socks.

Reva followed, grateful for the distraction—grateful she didn't have to be alone with Angad in that moment. Not just yet.

Angad waited outside while Reva made sure their teeth were brushed properly and their pajamas were on. He heard soft murmurs through the door—her voice, warm and patient, Avik whining about toothpaste flavor, Anika asking if Reva would stay the night.

A few minutes later, the kids emerged—fresh and still buzzing with excitement—as they scrambled back into the blanket fort, they'd half-made on the living room carpet.

Reva returned behind them. Her expression was neutral.

The twins snuggled in, ready for their story. Reva sank back onto the floor cushion, letting the twins pile onto either side of her. Avik handed her the book they'd picked—*The Adventures of Lenny the Lost Lollipop*.

Anika raised an eyebrow. "Again?"

"It's a classic," Avik replied with mock seriousness, earning a giggle from Anika.

Angad watched the three of them from his spot on the sofa. The lamp cast a soft amber glow over the room, catching the shine of Reva's hair as she tilted her head to read. Her voice wrapped around the words—sometimes silly, sometimes dramatic, sometimes with a gasp that made the twins squeal with delight.

The kids were entranced.

So was he.

And it scared the hell out of him.

Because in that moment, she wasn't just telling them a story. She was in their home. She was in their lives. And all he could think about was how easily she'd filled the space—how natural it felt having her there.

Her phone buzzed.

Reva glanced at the screen as it lit up and quickly picked it up. She answered, murmured a few words, then ended the call.

"It was Ramesh," she said softly, looking up at him. "Lata's train was on time. She's boarded safely."

Angad gave a small nod, relief loosening something in his chest.

"Good," he said, his voice softer now. "Thanks for checking."

She didn't reply, just gave him a small nod back—understated, distant. But the tension in the room softened by a fraction, like the silence had exhaled.

"...and then Lenny found his way back to the candy shop, where all the other sweets had been waiting for him, cheering him on with jellybean confetti."

Reva closed the book gently.

Anika leaned her head against her arm. "Best story ever."

Reva smiled, brushing a strand of hair from the girl's forehead.

"You say that every time," Avik said quietly. But then he yawned and continued, "But it really *was* the best this time because you read it, Reedi."

Reva's breath caught, her heart squeezing at the quiet weight of his words. She reached out instinctively, brushing Avik's hair back from his forehead as he yawned again, his eyes fluttering shut.

Angad felt something shift deep inside him. A mix of warmth and ache. Avik's words weren't loud, but they rang with the kind of honesty only kids were capable of. And they hit harder than anything else had in weeks.

Reva looked up, her eyes meeting Angad's for a fleeting second.

He held her gaze—soft, quiet, full of the things he still couldn't say.

Not yet.

Angad stood. "Come on, munchkins. Time to sleep."

They groaned in protest, but Reva stood with them. "Let me."

Angad watched her shepherd the twins to their rooms. She tucked Anika in, then lifted Avik into his bed—his eyes already half closed, a sleepy smile on his face. Her hands lingered a moment on his blanket before she stood up.

When she came out, Angad was standing near the bar in the living room, a drink in his hand, the bottle half uncorked beside him. His jaw was tight. His eyes blank.

"I'm heading out," she said, grabbing her tote bag.

"Wait."

She stopped mid-step.

He moved quickly, too quickly, cutting off her path at the front door.

"What are you doing?" she asked quietly, not looking at him.

"You didn't have to take over like this. I… I just…"

"I wasn't going to leave them alone, Angad. Lata *didi* had an emergency. I was there. That's it."

"Really?" His voice was low now, rough. "That's it?"

Before she could respond, her phone buzzed.

She pulled it out instinctively. The name flashing on the screen made his eyes narrow.

Rohit Arora.

He didn't speak. But she saw the flicker in his jaw.

The phone kept buzzing.

She silenced it.

"Take the call," he said, his voice like gravel.

"I'll call him later."

"Why not now?"

"Because I don't want to."

"Why not? Do you have something to hide?" he said with a dry laugh.

She tried to step past him. "I have to go."

The phone buzzed again.

"Take the call," he repeated, voice clipped.

She hesitated, then answered. "Hi, Rohit… no, I'm not free right now… yes, Monday should work."

She moved to the window as she spoke, her voice low, polite. At one point, she chuckled softly—an automatic response to something he said. It felt harmless.

But not to Angad. He stood near the front door, arms crossed, jaw clenched. Every word she spoke, every smile that wasn't his, grated on his insides.

She ended the call with a murmured, "Okay, see you then," and slipped the phone back into her bag.

He blocked her again.

"Angad—what are you doing?"

His eyes burned into hers. "Why are you meeting that man?"

She blinked. "Excuse me?"

"Rohit Arora. Why the hell do you need to meet him for?"

She drew herself up. "That's none of your business."

He took a step closer. "It *is* my business when you're meeting creeps who've hit on you at meetings."

"It's for work," she shot back. "And I don't need your permission."

"I told you to stay away from him."

"And you think you have the right to tell me who I can and can't meet?" she asked, voice cold. "That ended when I walked out of your apartment. The last time."

His chest rose and fell, rage and something else—hurt?—clashing in his eyes. "So you run to the first guy who—"

"Don't you dare say another word!" She cut him mid-sentence. Her voice was steel now. "I've run after enough people in my life. I won't chase another. Not him. And definitely not you!"

Silence. Thick. Heavy. Their breaths were the only sound between them. She looked away first.

"I'll see the kids tomorrow," she said as she reached for the door, and this time, he didn't stop her.

But his fingers tightened around the glass in his hand, and a thousand unsaid words burned behind his eyes.

***

CHAPTER TWENTY SIX

BOMBSHELL

Lata called a week after she left. Her voice was barely audible, thick with grief. Her mother passed away the night she had reached. The rituals would take time—at least fifteen to twenty days. Maybe more. She apologized over and over. Reva consoled her gently, offering words she knew would only skim the surface of comfort.

By then, a rhythm had set in.

Reva structured her mornings around the twins' school hours—client meetings before noon, quick grocery runs squeezed in between. She was always at the gate when school got over. The kids, used to her face by now, came running into her arms every afternoon. Lunch, homework, bath time, playtime—all became part of the new normal.

When Angad returned from work, he would find her there. Always. Tired but composed, calmly setting the dinner table or listening to the kids' chatter. They ate together like a family. But once the twins were asleep—tucked into bed with their favorite toys—Reva would quietly gather her things and leave.

There were no lingering conversations. No glances that lasted too long. No late-night silences to fill.

She didn't speak unless needed.

Like the day she handed him a circular from the school. "There's a parent-child sports event next Saturday," she said, voice even. "They want one guardian per child."

Angad took the note, their fingers brushing by accident. She didn't flinch, but her eyes didn't meet his either.

Then came the bombshell.

It started innocently enough.

Dinner was almost done—Raju had outdone himself with *roti*, *aloo-gobhi*, and chilled *dahi*, and the twins were unusually focused on their food. Their fingers were white with curd. Their plates were wiped clean like small battlefields after a happy war.

"Reedi," Anika said, licking her fingers and turning to Reva with wide eyes. "Do you know how many days are left for our birthday?"

Reva smiled, folding her napkin. "Wow… is your birthday coming up soon? When is it?"

"Third of August," Avik replied as if it were a national holiday that needed to be remembered by the entire country.

"Next week? Already?" Reva feigned shock. "No wonder there's a sparkle in the air!"

"Yes!" Anika bounced in her seat. "Daddy, can we have a party this year? At home? With balloons and music and return gifts?"

"Please, Daddy?" Avik chimed in, looking up at Angad with big, hopeful eyes.

Angad looked like someone had just handed him a live grenade wrapped in glitter. "Here? In the house?"

He blinked rapidly, clearly panicking. His brain was already processing logistics—guest lists, cleanup plans, cake size, noise complaints from neighbors. The man had handled media storms and high-stakes interviews with ease, but the idea of six-year-olds running amok in his living room had him visibly sweating.

Reva tried not to laugh. She glanced at him—Angad, the business tycoon who'd shifted his entire business base across continents without flinching, now looking as if someone had asked him to launch a rocket from his kitchen.

"I've managed primetime interviews with ministers and damage-control pressers for Fortune 500 CEOs," he muttered under his breath. "But glitter glue and themed balloons might just break me."

"Relax," Reva said with a soft chuckle. "Leave it to me."

Angad exhaled as if she'd just defused that grenade. "Thank God," he whispered dramatically.

"Okay, birthday planners," Reva clapped her hands. "Let's get started. First up: the guest list. Who's in? And what's the theme? Also, most important—what do you want as your birthday gift from *me*?"

"Cake!" Anika declared without missing a beat. "With a unicorn. And glitter on top!"

"No, no—superhero cake," Avik countered. "With Hulk *smashing* through the middle!"

"Fine," Anika conceded. "One of each."

"We want magic," Anika added. "And balloons that fall from the ceiling."

"And bubble guns," Avik piped up. "Can we have matching bubble guns, Reedi?"

Angad sat back in his chair, watching the three of them plan with more intensity than his finance team discussing quarterly projections. His home, which had been silent for so long, buzzed with energy and color. They moved from the dining table to the living room, still in discussion. Reva, seated cross-legged on the floor, scribbling ideas into a notebook, was somehow holding it all together.

He almost didn't hear the next thing Anika said.

"We also want gifts from you, Daddy."

Angad blinked. "Okay. What do you want?"

"Toys."

"Done."

"New Dresses."

"Done."

"We want Reedi to be our Mumma."

Silence.

Reva's pen froze mid-word.

Angad looked like someone who'd just watched his quarterly projections crash in real-time.

"You want *what*?" he asked slowly.

"Reedi should be our Mumma," Anika repeated like it was the most obvious thing in the world. "Vihaan said his Mumma picks him up from school, helps with his homework, and braids his hair."

"Helps him *study*," Avik corrected. "His Mumma doesn't braid *his* hair."

"But Bianca's Mumma does, like Reedi does mine," Anika continued. "She also planned her birthday party, chooses her dresses, and kisses her every night before sleeping."

"Exactly," Avik nodded. "You already do all that, Reedi. So why can't you just be our Mumma, too?"

Reva opened her mouth. Closed it again. There was a strange, invisible weight pressing against her chest.

She glanced at Angad—and what she saw in his eyes was enough to make her look away.

He was stunned. Speechless.

It wasn't just the question the kids had asked. It was the fact that, deep down, it had echoed something that had quietly taken root in both of them.

And now, it had found a voice—in the pure, innocent clarity of two six-year-olds who didn't care for complications or past heartbreaks.

They just knew what love looked like.

And to them, it looked like *Reedi.*

"We like it best when you're here," Avik added in a small voice. "It feels… good."

"And… happy," Anika finished.

Silence again. Thick. Drenched in unsaid emotion.

Reva placed the pen and notebook down carefully. Her hands trembled.

She looked at Angad again—and what she saw in his eyes made her heart stumble.

Panic. Ache. And something dangerously close to longing.

The air in the room thickened.

Reva opened her mouth, but no words came.

Angad couldn't look away from her.

The kids went back to discussing more birthday plans, oblivious to the tidal wave they'd just unleashed.

Reva finished the chores with a mechanical sort of calm, her fingers working on autopilot as she wiped the twins' mouths and handed them their water glasses. The children chattered about school, about Bianca and Vihaan, and some fight over a pink pencil, but all she could hear was that one question echoing like a pulse.

Why can't you just be our Mumma?

Later that night, once the kids had drifted off and the house had fallen into that familiar hush, Reva quietly gathered her bag.

Angad stood by the window, nursing his second drink. He hadn't said a word since dinner.

She didn't either.

But something had cracked open between them—something heavy and unspoken. And it followed her out the door, pressing against her chest as she stepped into the elevator.

*

Back at her apartment, Reva shut the door behind her and leaned against it, exhaling like she'd been holding her breath all evening. She didn't bother switching on the lights. The dim glow from the lights outside spilled faintly through the curtains, painting long shadows across the room.

She kicked off her sandals, one at a time, and sank onto the couch. The silence wrapped around her like a blanket—but not the comforting kind. This was the kind that echoed with everything unsaid, everything she'd pushed down, everything she didn't want to admit.

The home that usually felt like her sanctuary now felt hollow. Like she didn't quite belong here anymore. Or maybe… she'd just started belonging *somewhere else.*

Her phone buzzed on the coffee table, lighting up the dark.

Maa: *Are you home yet, beta?*

Reva stared at the screen. Her thumb hovered over the keyboard… but she didn't type. She tapped the green call button instead.

The phone rang once.

Twice.

Then— "Reva?"

She didn't speak. Not right away.

"Reva?" Naina's voice turned sharp with concern. "What's wrong?"

A breath escaped her lips—shaky, unsteady. "I don't know," she whispered. "Maybe... everything."

"I'm coming upstairs," her mother said immediately. No hesitation. No questions. The call cut off.

Barely a minute passed before the door opened. Naina stepped in, using the spare key Reva always insisted she keep in the drawer by her own kitchen.

She flicked on the light.

"Reva?"

Reva didn't say a word. She just looked up, her eyes glassy and rimmed red. And then she stood.

In two long steps, she crossed the room and buried herself in her mother's arms.

She didn't sob at first. It wasn't loud or dramatic. Just a silent, gut-deep ache that spilled out in the form of hot tears and trembling shoulders.

Naina wrapped her arms around her daughter, holding her the way she had when Reva was six and had lost her favorite toy. The way she had when Reva was sixteen and had come home after her first heartbreak. The way she had when Reva found the truth about Manish. And the way she did now—like there was nothing in the world she wouldn't hold together for her daughter if she could.

"Let it out," she whispered, stroking her daughter's hair. "Just breathe, *beta*. Let it out."

Reva did.

And when the worst of the wave had passed, when the sobs turned into hiccupped breaths and silent tears, she finally pulled back just enough to speak.

"I didn't mean to fall in love," she said softly, voice raw. "It just... happened."

Naina waited.

"I thought I was just helping them," Reva continued, pacing now, her hands restless, eyes distant. "Picking them up, making sure homework was done, making sure they ate properly. But somewhere between school runs and bedtime stories, they wrapped themselves around me."

She turned to her mother. "Maa, I know their food moods. I know Avik pretends to hate math but secretly loves the puzzle part. I know Anika can't sleep unless the nightlight is on and her stuffed bunny is right next to her. I tuck them in, and they reach for me before they even look for Angad."

She sank back into the couch. "I know I'm not their mother," she whispered. "But tonight... they asked me if I could be."

Naina was quiet for a beat.

Then, in that calm, wise voice that had guided Reva through every major and minor storm in her life, she asked, "And how did that feel?"

Reva gave a shaky laugh. "Like someone reached into my chest and cracked it open. Like... they found something I didn't know I was hiding."

Naina smiled gently, walking over and kneeling in front of her. "Reva, you're not just taking care of them. You *love* them. And children... they feel that. Purely. Instinctively. That's what they're responding to."

Reva blinked at her. "But that doesn't change anything, Maa. Angad doesn't love me. He's made that perfectly clear. I'm just—just someone helping out in an emergency. Nothing more."

Naina rolled her eyes like only a seasoned Indian mother could. "He knows nothing. Men are like that. Stupid in the ways that matter."

Reva let out a surprised chuckle, half-amused, half-heartbroken.

"I'm serious," Naina continued, straightening up. "That man looks at you like you hung the moon. And when you're not there? His eyes keep drifting to the door, waiting. Hoping."

Reva shook her head. "His kids are his only priority."

"And who do his kids want?"

Reva looked away because the answer was too loud in her heart. She didn't trust her voice to say it.

"They asked for you, Reva," Naina said gently. "They didn't ask for anyone else. They asked for *you*. That's not small. That's *everything.*"

Reva closed her eyes.

Everything.

And yet, she felt more uncertain than ever.

Because what if love wasn't enough?

What if *this* wasn't enough?

Or worse—what if it was everything she'd ever wanted... and she still couldn't have it?

*

Angad stood outside Anika's room first, one hand resting on the doorframe. The soft glow of her pink nightlight bathed the room in a warm hue, casting shadows over the stuffed unicorns that lined her shelf. She was curled up in the center of her bed, one arm flung across her bunny, the other hugging the corner of her blanket. Her lashes fluttered slightly as if she were deep in some magical dreamland she hadn't told anyone about yet.

He stepped in, slow and quiet, and tucked the blanket more securely around her. His fingers brushed her hair back from her forehead—her skin was warm, her breath steady.

A sense of peace. And yet, something was missing.

He stepped out and made his way down the hall to Avik's room.

This one was darker, the blue star projector casting constellations on the ceiling, blinking slowly. Avik was sprawled like a tiny superhero in training—one leg off the bed, his Avengers t-shirt twisted sideways, his hand still gripping a small toy car.

Angad chuckled softly and eased the car out of his fingers before it left a dent on his cheek. He adjusted the boy's blanket, too, his large hands gentle with habit now. He stood there a beat longer, staring at his son's face—so much like his own and yet so different. Softer. More open. Less scarred.

A sigh left his lips.

He stepped out, closing both doors halfway like Reva always did—just enough to let air in, but not so much that the hall light would wake them.

The house was still. Too still.

And her scent lingered.

That maddening, comforting mix of soft floral and vanilla clung to the air—woven into the fabric of the day, threaded through every hallway she'd walked down, every room she'd organized, every story she'd told. It was on the cushion that still had a faint indent where she'd leaned. It was in the half-folded towel in the bathroom. It was everywhere.

It was *her.*

He leaned against the wall for a moment, letting his head fall back with a quiet thud.

His mind was a mess of things—of memories, of words exchanged, of sharp silences and soft moments.

He could still hear her voice, firm and wounded:

"I won't chase another. Not him. And definitely not you."

And his own voice, rough with hurt and pride and the fear he couldn't name:

"So you run to the first guy who—"

He scrubbed a hand down his face. He'd screwed that up.

But even louder than all the anger and ache and regret were his daughter's words, spoken with the kind of innocence that left no room for evasion—

"We want Reedi to be our Mumma."

He hadn't had an answer then.

He still didn't.

But as he stood in the quiet corridor of a house that felt hollow without her laughter, without her voice weaving order into their chaos, without her fingers tucking the kids in...

He was starting to wonder if the kids weren't the only ones asking.

Maybe he was, too.

But could he be that selfish? Surely, she deserved better than him.

He didn't know.

But the ache in his chest told him that walking away from her again might just destroy him in ways nothing else ever had.

***

CHAPTER TWETY SEVEN

BLESSINGS

Angad woke up with her name on his lips.

Reva.

The sheets beside him were untouched, just like every morning before this. But today, they felt colder. Lonelier. There was a hollow ache in his chest—one that hadn't eased since the moment she'd walked out that day, her voice sharp and shaking as she declared she wouldn't chase him.

He hadn't slept much. Kept turning over, haunted by everything she'd said. And the things he hadn't. And then his thoughts turned to what had happened the night before.

"We want Reedi to be our Mumma."

She had looked up at him then—eyes wide, shimmering with unshed tears and questions she didn't voice. Questions he didn't dare answer.

He said nothing.

Not because he didn't feel anything.

But because he felt *too much.*

Because hope, when misplaced, could be crueler than silence. And Reva didn't deserve cruelty—not from him.

She wasn't thinking clearly, he told himself. She was overwhelmed. Wrapped in emotion, in the needs of his children, in a role she'd never asked for.

Someone had to think of her future.

Even if that future didn't include him.

Especially if it didn't.

He forced himself to move. He got up from the bed with every ounce of willpower he had left, putting one foot in front of the other, convincing himself he was doing the right thing—for *her*.

He made his way to the kitchen, poured himself a black coffee—burnt, bitter, just the way he deserved it.

And then the doorbell rang.

For one fleeting second, hope sparked.

Maybe...

Maybe she'd come back.

Maybe she—

He pulled the door open.

And standing there, beaming like it was the most ordinary Saturday in the world, was Naina.

Sunglasses perched on her head. A large tote slung over one shoulder.

"Good morning, Angad *beta*," she chirped like she owned the place.

Before he could say anything, the twins charged past his legs and into her arms. "Naniiii!" they screamed in delight. "You came! You really came!"

Angad blinked, still half-stunned. "Aunty...?"

"Nani is taking us shopping!" Anika announced, already hopping on one foot as she looked around for her other shoe. "For our birthday!"

"We're going to buy superhero T-shirts and party balloons!" Avik added excitedly, tugging Naina's hand.

"How... when did all this get planned?" Angad asked, still trying to piece it together.

Avik piped up, matter-of-fact, "Reedi called Raju Bhaiya in the morning. She said we should get ready because Nani was coming to take us shopping for our birthday!"

Naina looked up at Angad and offered a gentle smile. "Reva had a packed morning—meetings, deadlines, the usual. But she made sure these two little whirlwinds had a full day planned so you wouldn't have to worry." Her eyes twinkled as she added, "She thought they'd love some birthday shopping—and I could use the workout. You can pick them up in the evening, okay?"

And just like that, she turned with a breezy wave, herding the kids out the door as they yelled excited goodbyes over their shoulders.

The door clicked shut behind them, and Angad stood there, stunned.

She hadn't come. She hadn't called him. And he knew why.

But she hadn't left them either. Not really.

She made sure the kids weren't alone. That they were happy. Cared for. Distracted.

Loved.

A lump formed in his throat before he could swallow it down.

She was slipping away from him—not in grand declarations or dramatic silences, but in these small, intentional absences.

But even as she created space… she never truly left.

That was Reva.

And now, standing in his kitchen, holding a half-drunk cup of burnt coffee and a bruised heart, Angad knew he had to let her go completely.

He didn't want to.

Not when the kids still looked for her every day.

Not when the scent of her vanilla shampoo still lingered on his pillow.

Not when his heart beat with her name like a silent prayer.

But for her, he would.

He needed to see her. To talk to her. To explain.

Today.

And as if the universe had been waiting for his resolve, his phone buzzed.

It was Raj.

"Meet me at the club's private lounge if you're free in the evening, son," he said casually after the usual greetings.

Angad's heart sank a little as he hung up the call from her father, unease pooled in his stomach.

Maybe Raj wanted to warn him.

Tell him to keep his distance.

That Reva deserved better than a man with a past and two kids in tow.

He wouldn't argue. He was ready to agree. Apologize, even.

He stayed home through the day, alone with his thoughts, the silence settling over him like a heavy blanket. The hum of the refrigerator, the soft tick of the wall clock—everything felt louder in her absence. Her laughter no longer echoed down the hallway, and the house felt paused, mid-breath.

By evening, he slipped into jeans and a collared shirt, combed his hair with shaky fingers, and left the apartment—his heart in knots, his soul braced for impact.

Because if this really was goodbye…

He needed to hear it from her father first.

*

The private lounge was quiet. Cocooned in soft lighting and the faint hum of jazz, it was the kind of place meant for conversations that needed silence around them. Plush leather seats lined the room, and the scent of aged whiskey hung in the air.

Angad stepped in, still carrying the weight of the day on his shoulders.

Raj looked up from his seat by the corner, his eyes scanning Angad's face with the ease of someone who didn't need many words to know the story.

"You look like hell, son," Raj said dryly, though not unkindly. "What you need is a stiff drink."

A waiter appeared just then, almost on cue, placing two glasses of whiskey on the table alongside a tray of olives, roasted nuts, and small bites. Raj waited until they were alone again before gesturing for Angad to sit.

Angad sank into the chair opposite him, exhaling slowly.

Raj swirled the amber liquid in his glass before taking a sip. Then, after a beat, he leaned back, gaze steady.

"Tell me, Angad," he said, tone casual but laced with something deeper. "What did your parents ever tell you about Naina and me?"

Angad blinked. That… was not the question he expected.

He thought back for a moment before speaking. "Honestly… not much. They just said they'd made new friends—you and Naina Aunty. That they liked you both a lot." He gave a faint smile. "My mom called you a breath of fresh air. And she was right. In a world full of pretense and polished masks, you are real. The kind of real most people have forgotten how to be."

He paused, the memory softening his voice.

"Maa used to say it felt like she'd known Naina Aunty her whole life. Like, there was an ease there that didn't need explaining."

Another pause.

"And the last time I spoke to them... they said the next time I came to India, they'd introduce me to your family." His throat tightened. "That's all."

Raj gave a soft nod, the weight of memory settling over his features.

"Let me tell you what your parents told us—what they truly wanted."

He leaned back, swirling the amber liquid in his glass.

"The day they met Reva, they were smitten. They may have met her only once or twice, but Renu would often tell Naina, *'One day, I'm going to make that girl my daughter.'*"

He chuckled softly at the memory.

"She was half-joking, of course. She used to say, *'You take our Angad, and I'll take your Reva!'*"

Angad sat still, blindsided by the revelation.

"When they died so suddenly in that crash," Raj went on, his voice heavier now, "and we lost contact with you. Any hope of that ever happening vanished with them. And then..."

He paused meaningfully. "Manish happened."

Angad's jaw clenched. The name hit like a bruise.

"We never liked him," Raj said plainly. "But Reva... she thought the world of him. That's who she is. Always sees the best in people—even when they least deserve it. We agreed to the match because she seemed happy. And then that man—"

His voice tightened. "—that leech cheated on her. Broke her in a way I'd never seen before. She lost faith. In love. In herself. In her worth."

He took a long sip of whiskey before continuing, more quietly now.

"It's been years. And while she's rebuilt parts of herself, I don't think she ever truly returned to who she was... not until now."

Raj looked up, meeting Angad's gaze with quiet intensity.

"I know I'm her father, and maybe that makes me biased. But that girl... she doesn't even realize how precious she is."

Raj paused, his voice softening.

"The day I saw you walk out of her kitchen... it all came rushing back. I recognized you instantly—Omi's son."

He smiled faintly, a glimmer of something tender in his eyes.

"And in that moment, all my worries about Reva disappeared. I knew she'd be fine. That she'll be in good hands."

Angad looked down at his glass. Hands clenched.

"But Uncle," Angad said quietly, the weight of his fears finally finding a voice. "I'm not just someone's son anymore... I'm also a father. I come with a past. With responsibilities. With kids." He hesitated, then added, "Surely, this isn't the kind of future you want for her."

Raj gave a small smile, his voice calm but sure.

"Have you seen her with the kids, Angad? She lights up when they laugh. It's not just affection—it's something deeper."

He paused, his gaze steady.

"When we came back from Mumbai, she asked about Avik more times than I could count. *'Did he get a fever after the fall?' 'Was he sleeping okay?' 'Did he cry at night?'* She couldn't stop worrying. Her heart is already with them."

He leaned back slightly, thoughtful.

"She doesn't see them as someone else's children. She sees them as her own. Not because she has to… but because she *wants* to."

Raj let the words hang between them for a beat, then added quietly,

"I know it's unconventional, especially in our society. But I'm not worried about the damn society. My only concern is my daughter's happiness."

He met Angad's eyes.

"You're a father, too. You understand." He paused and then asked, "So, tell me—where does your kids' happiness lie?"

Angad swallowed. Words wouldn't form.

Raj leaned in. "You're scared. I get that. But forget the practicalities for a moment. Ask yourself the only question that matters: Do you love her?"

Angad's throat burned. His eyes glistened. He nodded.

Raj's eyes crinkled. "Then go tell her that. You have our blessings. And your parents' blessings, too. And don't worry about the kids—let the grandparents spoil them for a bit. I'm pretty sure Naina has already tricked them into a sleepover."

Right on cue, Angad's phone buzzed—a video call from Naina.

He answered. The twins popped into view, bouncing.

"Daddy! Can we *please* stay at Nanu-Nani's tonight? Nani was very sad. She said she missed us after Mumbai," Anika pouted dramatically.

Raj laughed and took the phone. "Of course you can. Your daddy agrees."

He handed the phone back to Angad, who smiled and nodded in response. The twins squealed in delight before the call ended.

Raj handed him a key.

"Reva's not home at the moment. Here's the spare key to her apartment. Go. I'll make sure Naina sends her there."

Angad stood, suddenly breathless.

He hugged Raj tightly, whispered a choked "Thank you," and rushed out.

Towards his future. His life. His Reva.

***

CHAPTER TWENTY EIGHT

COMING HOME

The key trembled slightly in Angad's hand as he opened the door to her apartment. It was quiet inside, dimly lit, faintly scented with lavender and something unmistakably hers.

He stepped in slowly, his heart pounding like it hadn't in years. His eyes scanned the living room—neat, familiar, filled with little touches that were so completely Reva. The stack of books by the couch. Her favorite throw blanket crumpled in the corner. A half-burned vanilla candle on the side table. All of it whispered home.

And then he heard it—the soft rustle of footsteps from the hallway.

The door clicked shut behind her as Reva stepped inside, wearing faded jeans and an oversized tee that hung loose around her frame, the fabric slightly wrinkled from the long day. Her hair was twisted into a messy knot, more functional than style, with a few strands plastered to her temple from dried sweat or tears—maybe both.

Her glasses perched low on her nose, doing a poor job of concealing the swollen redness around her eyes. Her skin looked blotchy, her lips pressed tightly together like she'd been holding back sobs for hours. She didn't look up at first—just let the silence close around her like a tired sigh. She looked like someone who'd finally made it home after pretending to be okay all day—and failing.

And then she saw him.

"Angad?" Her voice was barely above a whisper. "What—how did you—?"

He didn't speak immediately. He simply looked at her.

Really looked.

Not just at the tear-reddened eyes behind her glasses or the tired set of her shoulders—but at everything she carried in her silence.

The woman who had held his children when they cried, not flinching from their grief or their chaos.

The woman who knew how to calm Anika's stormy tantrums with just a soft word and a tighter hug, and who understood the quiet codes Avik used to hide his hurt.

The woman who had quietly stepped into his well-ordered world and, without asking for space, made room for herself.

Who didn't change anything—but somehow made everything feel different.

The woman who made his house feel fuller, softer.

The home that was not cold, not broken. Just… missing something. Until her.

And now, standing in front of him with messy hair, no makeup, and the truth of her pain etched raw on her face, she looked more beautiful than ever. Not because she was trying—but because she wasn't.

Because she had nothing left to hide.

"I thought it was better this way," he started, voice barely above a whisper. "To push you away. To act like it didn't mean anything. To keep you out of the mess I call life."

Reva didn't say a word. She stood still—arms wrapped tightly across her chest like she was holding herself together.

"I told myself I was protecting you," he continued, eyes never leaving her face. "Protecting you from the late nights and tantrums and doctors and school runs. From the exhaustion, the chaos, the weight of it all."

He paused, his breath catching. "But the truth is… I wasn't protecting you. I was protecting *me*."

His voice cracked on that last word.

"Because I wanted you. So damn much. More than I've wanted anything in years. And that terrified me. Wanting you for myself felt selfish. Wanting you for *them* felt even worse."

He took a shaky step closer.

"I kept thinking—what kind of man does that? What kind of man asks a woman like you to give up her quiet mornings, her clean life, her freedom… for a man who's already lived a thousand lifetimes? Who comes with shadows, with wounds, with children who've never even known what having a mother feels like? Until you came along."

He dragged a hand through his hair, restless, broken open.

"There are no off days. No weekends either. It's all me. It's always been just me," he said, his voice rough with truth. "And I didn't want to trap you in that. Didn't want you to wake up one day and realize you signed up for a life that wasn't even fully yours."

He paused, eyes searching hers, voice thickening with guilt.

"That day… when Avik fell, and I missed the calls—" he exhaled sharply, "—I panicked. I was terrified. Not just because he was hurt, but because I realized how thin I was stretched. How easily things could fall apart. I thought… if I gave even a little more of myself to you, I'd be failing them. And if I gave everything to them, I'd be failing you."

He swallowed hard, the ache clear in his eyes.

"My kids have always been my priority. They had to be. And I told myself it wouldn't be fair to let you come second. You deserve more. You deserve to be someone's first priority. To be loved fully, with nothing held back."

He looked down for a moment, then back at her.

"I see it now. You weren't asking to be first. You were just asking to be seen. You just wanted a place beside me, a space in the life I was already living. You were ready to take it all on—my kids, my fears, my mess. And I... I kept turning you away."

His eyes locked with hers, vulnerable and aching.

"What I didn't see—what I was too damn scared to admit—was that *you were already in*. In every bedtime story, in every whispered 'Reedi' that came from their lips. You were in the quiet moments, the loud ones, the chaos, and the calm. You didn't just step into our lives, Reva. You *became* part of us."

He stepped closer still, his voice now shaking with emotion.

"I kept telling myself that protecting you meant letting you go. That I was doing the right thing by staying away. But it wasn't—it was just the easier thing. Easier than facing the truth…"

A pause, breathless.

"…That I am in love with you."

Reva's lips parted, but no sound came. She stood still, barely breathing.

"You don't get to say that," she whispered, voice thick with emotion. "Not after everything."

Angad flinched, but she didn't stop.

"You don't get to stand here now and tell me you love me—after shutting me out, after making me feel like I didn't belong. Like there was never going to be room for me in your life, no matter how hard I tried to make space."

Her voice trembled, rising despite her efforts to steady it.

"I wasn't asking you to choose between me and your kids. I just wanted to *be chosen*. To be let in. To be part of your world."

Pain flared in her eyes as she met his gaze. "But every time I tried to get close, you built another wall. Every time I stayed, you reminded me—without saying a word—that this life wasn't mine to dream about. That I could hold your children when they cried, but not be allowed to love them. That I could stand next to you in the dark, but never be part of your morning."

"I walked away because I thought you didn't want me," she continued, voice cracking. "That you didn't trust me to love you *and* your children. That you didn't see me… not in the real sense."

She took a shaky breath, her lips trembling now. "But I also kept showing up. Not for the hope of a promise. But because I love them. And I love *you*. I didn't ask for perfect. I just wanted *you* to choose me."

Her voice trembled as she spoke, the weight of weeks crashing into a single moment.

"And every time you didn't… it broke something in me."

Tears slipped silently down her cheeks now, trailing warmth down skin gone cold with memory. But she didn't look away.

"I know," he whispered, his own eyes rimmed with tears. "And I'm sorry. I'm so sorry."

She swallowed hard, fighting the lump that had lodged in her throat for far too long.

"You told yourself you were protecting me. But in reality…" Her voice cracked. "You walked away when it started to matter. When *we* started to matter."

Her shoulders shook as tears welled again—unchecked, unhidden this time.

"And the worst part is—I understood," she whispered. "I understood why you pulled back. Why you hesitated."

Her breath hitched, but she powered through.

"I told you I've stopped chasing people who don't want me. And yet, I stayed. I waited. I kept coming back… because something in me refused to give up. Because I loved you."

A sob rose and escaped, broken and raw.

"I loved *them*."

Her voice fractured, barely more than a whisper now.

"And you kept pretending that wasn't real. That my heart was something I could just… take back."

A beat of silence stretched between them, ragged and trembling.

"But I can't," she whispered. "I don't *want* to."

He took a step toward her, but she didn't move. Just kept looking at him like he held every piece of her still-beating heart in his hands.

"So, if you're here just because you're scared of losing me… don't," she said, her voice quiet but steady. "I was always here, even when you made it hard to stay. But I won't keep waiting to be chosen. Not again. If you want me… *really* want me—then show me. Mean it."

She took a breath, her eyes never leaving his.

Angad looked at her like the ground had shifted under his feet.

"I love you," he said again, his voice breaking now. "Not because you fit into my life. But because without you… nothing fits anymore. And if you'll have me, I'll spend the rest of my life showing you I mean it."

Reva's lips parted, then pressed together as if holding a thousand unsaid things. Her eyes shimmered with everything she'd carried and everything she still dared to hope.

And then she stepped forward.

Reached up.

Pulled him into a kiss that tasted like salt and redemption—like every goodbye they'd barely survived and every homecoming they didn't dare believe in.

His hands buried in her hair. Her fingers curled into his shirt. Everything poured into that moment—every ache, every longing, every stubborn shard of love that had never really left.

It was fierce.

It was forgiving.

And it was forever.

Because this time, there were no questions left.

Only answers.

Only them.

***

EPILOGUE

One Year Later.

The Sareen residence was buzzing with quiet chaos.

Reva stood in the middle of it all, a hand on her hip. She was dressed in denim shorts and a T-shirt that read *"Chief Chaos Coordinator."* Her hair was twisted in a loose bun, glitter smudged on her cheek, and a cup of tea in the other hand. Her glasses slid down her nose, and her voice carried through the rooms like a general on a battlefield.

The twins tore through the living room like mini tornadoes, leaving behind stray socks, a feather boa, and one very 'exhausted' balloon dog.

"Avik! You cannot wear mismatched shoes just because they're both blue! And Anika, the unicorn tiara is for the party, not before!"

"Why can't unicorns come to birthday parties, Mumma?" Anika came running to her.

"Because they live in a magical land, sweetheart," she explained, gently prying a ribbon from Anika's hair before it got knotted further. "And also, they're imaginary."

Anika tilted her head, unconvinced. "Daddy said you were magical, too. But you're here."

Reva blinked, momentarily caught off guard. "Well. That's... different magic," she said with a sheepish smile.

Just then, Avik burst in from the kitchen, holding a lopsided cookie. "Mumma! Raju bhaiya says this is a lion, but it looks like a potato. Can you tell him?"

She took the cookie and inspected it with exaggerated seriousness. "Hmm. Definitely a potato. But a *fierce* one."

Satisfied, Avik ran off again, leaving a trail of crumbs and chaos behind him.

In the kitchen, Lata moved with practiced ease, helping Raju sort the party snacks and tag the return gifts, her sari *pallu* tucked in tightly, eyes sharp, hands swift. She tutted at the glitter mess on the floor but said nothing—after all, it was birthday week, and glitter was the least of their worries.

From the hallway, Angad watched the whole thing unfold—the messy joy of it, the ease with which she'd become *theirs*.

They'd gotten married soon after he'd proposed—a small ceremony, just family, close friends, and two very excited six-year-olds who, upon hearing the news, had looked at each other wide-eyed before blurting, *"Will Reedi be living with us forever now?"* and *"Is she our Mumma now?"*

"Mumma," the kids called her now, so naturally, it didn't catch him off guard anymore—nor did it sting with guilt. The first time it had happened, Reva had turned around slowly, stunned and teary-eyed. That night, she cried into his chest and told him it felt like she'd finally earned something she didn't even know she'd been longing for.

She hadn't missed a school meeting or a doctor's visit in a year. She had a special knock to enter their room, a name for each of their favorite stories, and a magic touch that could undo Anika's moods and Avik's sulks. They adored her. And Angad? He was headlong in love—still, again, always.

"You know," he said as the twins dashed off down the hall again, leaving a trail of giggles and mismatched socks, "if I didn't know any better, I'd think I was a guest in *your* house."

Reva looked up from her cup of *chai*, brow raised. "Jealous, Mr. Sareen?"

"Just a little, Mrs. Sareen," he murmured, strolling into the living room and wrapping his arms around her from behind. "They don't even come to me with sock emergencies anymore. Or snack bribes. Or hairband negotiations. I've been… replaced."

She smirked, but her body softened into his. "Well, maybe it's because you already had your turn. You raised them this far."

"Oh?" he said, pressing a kiss to her temple. "And you're claiming them now?"

"Absolutely," she replied, turning in his arms. "These two are mine."

"I mean, that's debatable…" he teased.

She grinned, tapping his chest with a sparkle in her eye. "But the *next* one's all yours."

He stared at her, momentarily thrown.

She lifted her brows. "You've got more experience with newborns, remember? You're the seasoned pro, and I'm the rookie. So—congratulations, Daddy. You're on diaper duty."

Angad blinked. Twice.

Then, his mouth parted in disbelief. "Wait! What?"

Reva nodded slowly, her smile gentle. "It's still early, but… yeah."

He stared at her like the news had tilted his whole world—but in the best possible way. His arms tightened around her, awe painted across his features.

"We're having a baby," he whispered.

"We are. And with *your* track record, who knows? Maybe two," she said, grinning at his stunned expression. "And just like last time, *you're* the one having sleepless nights."

He laughed, breathless, before leaning down to kiss her, slow and full of wonder.

From the hallway, a loud crash interrupted the moment, followed by Avik's voice yelling, "Mummaaaa! Anika poured glitter into my shoes again!"

Reva sighed, already pulling away.

"Yours," Angad called after her with a grin. "Both of them. Officially."

She glanced back over her shoulder with a smirk. "Enjoy your peace while it lasts, Sareen. You've got about eight months left."

And then she disappeared into the joyful chaos of their lives, barefoot and glowing, and *his*, as balloons swayed above them, cake boxes on the countertop, and love filled every room in their home—multiplying by the minute.

The End

ABOUT THE AUTHOR

Ritu Khurana brings over two decades of experience in the field of education, coupled with a strong foundation in the corporate sector. During the COVID-19 pandemic, she returned to her lifelong love for books and transitioned into professional editing—an interest she had nurtured informally for years. Since then, she has worked on a range of fiction and non-fiction titles as an editor, helping shape compelling narratives and clear communication. This debut novel marks her entry into fiction writing, where her eye for detail, deep empathy, and love for storytelling come together to create an engaging and emotionally resonant read.